Avery's pulse started to thump. What did he want? And why on earth should she feel excited?

Ten minutes ago she'd been angry, on her way home with a clear conscience. It was simpler this way. So why had she felt so very glad to see him striding across the pavement?

"She's mine," he blurted out.

That was not what Avery had expected. "I beg your pardon?"

His face softened. "She looks exactly like my baby sister did at that age. Today's appointment…it's a formality, Avery. I know she's mine. I've known it deep down for a few days now."

Avery's thoughts jumbled together. He had a sister? Callum was so gruff and solitary it seemed impossible to think of him surrounded by parents and siblings. And yet she knew he hadn't just hatched, fully formed, as the broody recluse he seemed to be.

And then there was the heady fact that without proof he was actually acknowledging that Nell was his daughter.

She was happy about that. And scared as hell, too. The same feelings she'd had that first day came rushing back. Afraid of what he might demand. Afraid of ⸻ g in her life.

Dear Reader

Do you have sisters? Aren't they great? I mean, every now and again they make you want to pull your hair out or maybe roll your eyes, but when push comes to shove…

My sisters are quite a bit older than I am, and I'm sure when we were all (ahem…) much younger there were times they wished I would just disappear. Like when they had dates and I wanted to tag along so I didn't miss anything (honestly, I was like a bad rash they couldn't get rid of!). Or when they started taking on adult responsibilities and the baby of the family seemed overly privileged (Who? Me?).

But there are other times when only a sister will do. Your sister always has your back. Your sister is one of the few people who can share the family memories you've gathered your whole life. Your sister will cry with you and your sister will make you cry with laughter. Your sister will keep your secrets. In short: there's nothing like a sister.

Which brings me to the current heroine of this book: Avery. Avery misses her sister Crystal so much. They were best friends, confidantes. Avery's lost without Crystal, and the only thing keeping her going is raising her baby niece, Nell. Having Nell is like having a little bit of her sister there with her. Being a good mom is the most important thing in her life, so dealing with Nell's father, Callum, becomes a bit tricky. Especially when she finds herself falling for him…

I thought about my sisters a lot while writing this story, and baby Nell is named after my own sister, Janell. I wonder if she will grow up to have the same twinkle in her eye and wicked sense of humour that my sister has?

Warmest wishes

Donna

LITTLE COWGIRL ON HIS DOORSTEP

BY
DONNA ALWARD

First published in Great Britain 2013
by Mills & Boon, an imprint of Harlequin (UK) Limited.
Harlequin (UK) Limited, Eton House, 18-24 Paradise Road, Richmond, Surrey TW9 1SR

© Donna Alward 2013

ISBN: 978 0 263 23438 1

Harlequin (UK) policy is to use papers that are natural, renewable and recyclable products and made from wood grown in sustainable forests. The logging and manufacturing process conform to the legal environmental regulations of the country of origin.

Printed and bound in Great Britain
by CPI Antony Rowe, Chippenham, Wiltshire

A busy wife and mother of three (two daughters and the family dog), **Donna Alward** believes hers is the best job in the world: a combination of stay-at-home mum and romance novelist. An avid reader since childhood, Donna always made up her own stories. She completed her arts degree in English literature in 1994, but it wasn't until 2001 that she penned her first full-length novel and found herself hooked on writing romance. In 2006 she sold her first manuscript, and now writes warm, emotional stories for Mills & Boon® Cherish™.

In her new home office in Nova Scotia, Donna loves being back on the east coast of Canada after nearly twelve years in Alberta, where her career began, writing about cowboys and the West. Donna's debut romance, HIRED BY THE COWBOY, was awarded the Bookseller's Best Award in 2008 for Best Traditional Romance.

With the Atlantic Ocean only minutes from her doorstep, Donna has found a fresh take on life and promises even more great romances in the near future!

Donna loves to hear from readers. You can contact her through her website, www.donnaalward.com, her page at www.myspace.com/dalward, or through her publisher.

Books by Donna Alward:

THE REBEL RANCHER
THE LAST REAL COWBOY
HOW A COWBOY STOLE HER HEART
A FAMILY FOR THE RUGGED RANCHER
HONEYMOON WITH THE RANCHER

Other titles by this author are available in eBook format.
Visit www.millsandboon.co.uk

To my sisters

CHAPTER ONE

HE HAS A face that could frighten small children.

That was the first thing that sprang to Avery Spencer's mind as she stared up at the imposing figure of Callum Shepard. With his stubbled face and long tangle of hair, he didn't look anything like the clean-cut, charismatic groomsman she'd met just over a year ago. And definitely not the image of a doting dad, she thought with dismay. He stood with feet spread wide, one broad hand splayed on the edge of the door, glowering down at her like she'd committed a cardinal sin.

Except if anyone was the sinner here, it was him. And she reminded herself of that fact to keep from being intimidated—as surely that was his intent. She felt the first tiny trickle of sweat sneak down her spine in the cloying summer heat. Everyone always said Alberta was a *dry* heat, but that sure wasn't keeping her shirt from sticking to her back. It made her shift uncomfortably just at the moment she needed to be in absolute control. This could go so wrong in so many ways....

"What do you want?" he asked sharply.

Apparently he had also acquired the manners of a boor. How lovely. For a brief second Avery considered that making this trip might have been a colossal mistake. But then she squared her shoulders and lifted her chin. No, it had been the right thing to do. At least after today there would no longer be any secrets or lies. She wouldn't spend the rest of her life looking over her shoulder wondering what would happen if he ever found out about Nell. Far better to face it head-on and get it over with.

Besides, when it came down to brass tacks, Avery really believed that Nell deserved to know both parents. She swallowed, battling against the familiar wave of grief whenever she thought of her sister, Crystal. In this case, Nell deserved to get to know the one true parent she had left. Callum.

"You don't remember me, do you, Mr. Shepard?"

His dark brows pulled together. "Should I?"

That stung. After all, she remembered him, and he'd looked far different the last time she'd seen him, which was one year, one month and…what, five days ago? Not that she was counting, mind you. Back then his hair had been precisely cut, his face clean-shaven and he'd been wearing a suit with a single white rose in the lapel. Avery's tongue snuck out and licked across her dry lips. She knew that because the moment he'd stepped into the hotel suite she'd looked up and her mouth had gone dry and her palms sweaty. Callum Shepard had been gorgeous. And when he'd smiled, her stomach had gone all swirly.

Even when he'd looked right past Avery and his gaze had fallen on her sister.

Now his hair hung in straggly waves down to his collar, he looked as if he hadn't shaved in two days and his plaid shirt was only half tucked into old jeans. And smile? More like permanent scowl. The change was remarkable—and disheartening considering the circumstances. Not to mention incredibly intimidating.

Being intimidated wouldn't suit at all, not if she were to stay in control of the situation as she planned. "I'm Avery

Spencer." She held out her hand, determined to meet the task ahead with politeness and a modicum of grace.

His face stayed blank and his hand stayed beside his thigh. Not much surprise that it didn't sound familiar, she supposed. After all, he'd only had eyes for Crystal that weekend. He probably hadn't given Avery a second glance. Why would he?

"It doesn't ring a bell, sorry." And still he stood in the middle of the doorway. No invitation to come in, no nothing. Gatekeeper, lord and master of his own domain. She lowered her hand again, feeling foolish.

"We met in Niagara Falls last year."

Ah, she thought with satisfaction. A flicker of *something* passed over his face. Avery swallowed and added, "At Pete and Elizabeth's wedding."

His dark eyes settled on her, so intense it made her want to fidget. She clenched her fingers together and made herself remain still.

"You were there?" he asked.

If that was an attempt to make her feel insignificant, it succeeded. Was she so plain that she wasn't even the least bit noticeable? The slightest bit memorable? Granted, she'd never been as beautiful as her sister and whenever they were together, Avery did tend to fade into the background next to Crystal's perfect figure and pretty face. But confirmation that he didn't remember at all...

Ouch.

"I was in the wedding party," she explained, wishing she could just tell him her reason for showing up and get it over with. But she had to ease into it. Especially since she hadn't really been afforded so much as a smile or welcome. This was going to be so much harder than she'd imagined, and she'd practiced the words in her head over and over on the flight from Toronto to Edmonton, and from the drive from Edmonton to Cadence Creek. Now those words didn't seem to fit the situation at all.

"You were?"

Why did he keep questioning everything she said? Annoyance flickered and she struggled to tamp it down. She had to keep a lid on her temper. Calm and rational was the only way to get through this first meeting.

"I was one of Elizabeth's bridesmaids. You were Pete's best man." She tried a smile, hoping to soften him a touch. A slight breeze ruffled her blouse, offering a tiny bit of relief from the blazing heat. There weren't even any shade trees to offer respite from the sun, just green and brown fields surrounding the rather plain farmhouse, broken only by a large barn and a couple of sheds.

"Yes, I think I can remember that much," he said, a touch impatiently.

Avery looked over her shoulder, glancing back at the car she'd rented at the airport. So far Nell hadn't made a peep—but that wouldn't hold out forever. She was glad now that she'd chosen to leave Nell in the car, considering Shepard's convenient amnesia about the weekend in question. But time was ticking. The window was rolled all the way down, but it was too hot to leave the baby in the car for more than a few minutes.

She turned back, deciding they were getting nowhere and she might as well step it up. "You probably don't remember me because you were pretty interested in my sister," she stated plainly. "Crystal."

Something lit in his eyes. So he did remember. She wasn't surprised. It was hard to forget Crystal Spencer once you'd met her. Pain flickered at the thought. Avery's sister had been the brightest light in her life. Her death had been sudden and shocking, only a few days after giving birth to Nell. Avery had been plunged into darkness, losing her only real family.

But the darkness only lasted for a short time. Nell had become the new light in her life. Her saving grace.

"I remember your sister," he said, a touch of caution in his voice. "But that doesn't explain why you're knocking on my door…what did you say your name was, again?"

"Avery," she repeated firmly. "My name is Avery."

"Right. Look, if this is about Crystal, we had an understanding from the start. It was a weekend thing. No expectations."

Avery noticed he ran his hand through his hair, though, like he wasn't quite as cool about everything as he'd first appeared. And Avery was quite aware that the terms of the weekend had been set out from the start. Crystal had made that abundantly plain each time Avery tried to convince her to try to find Callum. Each time Crystal had flatly refused to budge. She'd been determined to raise Nell on her own. She didn't want some here-today-gone-tomorrow soldier as a father to her child. Especially since they barely knew each other.

Avery had never judged Crystal for how she'd conceived Nell. But she had judged her for willingly keeping silent about her pregnancy. Avery still believed that Callum deserved to know, but she wished she could take back the things she'd said to her sister.

"Crystal is dead, Mr. Shepard."

His hand dropped to his side as silence fell around them. Avery swallowed around the thickness in her throat. Saying the words never got easier.

"I'm so sorry," he said quietly, his voice a low rumble, and his gaze softened. It was the first sign of humanity she'd glimpsed in him.

"I don't know how else to put this, so I'm just going to

say it," she said, taking a deep breath and thinking a quick, silent prayer for strength. She was going to need it in the hours…in the days…ahead. "Crystal died shortly after delivering a baby. *Your* baby, Mr. Shepard. She's sleeping in the car behind me, and she's just over four months old."

Callum heard the words but they seemed to swim around in his head, not fitting together right. Crystal…Niagara Falls…baby.

But they'd been careful…hadn't they?

There had to be some mistake. He couldn't be a father. He remembered Avery, all right. He'd been flat-out lying about that part, not wanting to give himself away. At the first glimpse of her he'd flashed back to a memory of the bridesmaids, all lined up in dresses the color of a peacock feather. She'd been there, all right, an understated beauty next to the flashier glamour of her sister. At the time he'd thought her fresh and innocent. Perfect. And intimidating as hell.

But that didn't mean Avery was telling the whole story. After all, most scams succeeded because they carried a whiff of truth, just enough to be credible. Her presence here rattled him, so he held his cards close to his chest.

"I'm not a father," he heard himself say. "It's impossible."

"I assure you it's not," she repeated. "You did have sex with my sister that weekend, didn't you?" She blinked at him innocently. "You'll notice I refrain from using the term 'making love' as I'm relatively sure love had nothing to do with it. Considering you'd just met and then never contacted her again."

Her reprimand broke through the haze in his mind and he tightened his fingers around the door. Lord, she was a piece of work. Righteousness all wrapped up in a tidy little package of uptight conservatism—from her tailored white trousers to her buttoned-up blouse with the scarf precisely knotted—just so—around her neck. His gaze dropped to her shoes. Little heels, not too high, of course. Nothing that smacked of outright sex appeal for this woman. Oh, he had her pegged, all right. Or at least the part she was playing.

He certainly didn't trust her enough yet to know if it was all an act or not. For all he knew, Crystal was fine and dandy. Or maybe this was Avery's kid and she was out to scam him for child support.

For the first time since opening the door, he felt his lips curve slightly. If she was after bags of money she was barking up the wrong tree. He'd sunk every dime he had into buying this place and the milk quota that went along with it. All he wanted from life now was to be left alone. To live his life on this quiet section of land with the open space and some livestock for company.

"Is something entertaining?" she asked, pursing her lips.

"Not a bit," he replied. "In fact, I don't believe a single word out of your mouth. I suggest you turn around and head back to where you came from."

And if his conscience dug at him a little bit, he would just damn well ignore it.

He stepped inside and shut the door in her face.

Only when it was latched did he close his eyes. He pressed his forehead to the door and let out a long, unsteady breath. This was not happening. It was not. Yes, he'd had a fling over a year ago, but it had been a bad time for him. Jane had broken things off and given him back the ring, destroying his hopes for the future. He'd wanted to be anywhere but at a wedding, pretending to celebrate a happy-ever-after he no longer believed in. Crystal had been the perfect diversion. But surely Elizabeth would have mentioned if her maid of honor had ended up pregnant. Women were close like that, weren't they?

But then he remembered that after the wedding, Elizabeth had moved to Quebec with Pete, hundreds of kilometers away from Crystal Spencer. They'd only been married a few months when Pete—along with Callum and the rest of their section—had been deployed.

Callum had been the only one of them to make it home. That fact still made his guts churn.

Through the wood he heard the slam of her car door. She was going, then. It was just as well. Callum Shepard wasn't anyone's father.

The sharp knock vibrated through his forehead and made him stand straight up. Not going. With a sigh he prepared to let her know in no uncertain terms that he wasn't playing her game. He opened the door and...

And stared, swallowing the words sitting on his tongue.

Avery cradled a tiny bundle in her arms, a still-sleeping bundle, wrapped in a soft yellow knitted blanket with only her head poking out of the folds. Tiny lips were surrounded by plump cheeks; the tiniest button nose dotted the middle of her face and dark hair showing just a hint of curl peeked out from beneath a tiny pink-and-white bonnet.

As much as he hated to admit it, it was hard to keep such a hard stance when the baby was right there in front of him rather than stashed away in a car.

"Miss Spencer," he began, more affected than he cared to admit, "I know what you're doing. You're playing the cute baby card."

"Is it working?"

Avery's clear blue eyes actually looked hopeful. Before they'd only held hostility and derision. She'd judged him for indulging in a brief affair with her sister. Why would she feel the need to do that if she were lying about him being the father? She was either telling the truth or she was an extraordinarily good liar.

Fortunately—or unfortunately, depending how one looked at it—he been burned before. Burned badly enough that he didn't trust himself to know the difference. No matter how much those extraordinary blue eyes implored him to believe her.

"Cute or not, I'm going to need more proof than your say-so," he answered. Yet he couldn't pull his gaze away from the fringe of dark hair. Avery was blonde. Crystal had been blonde. The baby had dark brown hair, like his.

Which proved absolutely nothing, he reminded himself.

"Could we at least come in?" she asked softly. "It's silly to be standing on your doorstep." She fluttered her hand. "The mosquitoes are out and I don't want Nell getting bit."

"Nell?"

Avery nodded. "Short for Janell. It was the name of Crystal's nurse at the hospital."

Something strange passed over Avery's face as she said the words. Callum's jaw tightened as he recognized the emotion. Pain. Grief. Lord knew he was familiar enough with them both. The longer this conversation went on, the more he was inclined to think she might be telling the truth.

He wondered what had happened to Crystal. He'd barely known her, but he did have enough humanity left in his soul to feel sorry she was gone. And to feel sorry for Avery, who had clearly loved her.

Reluctantly he stood back and pushed the door open. "Come on in, then. Don't mind the mess."

She'd soon learn that he came just as he was. And that would have her leaving soon enough.

* * *

Callum Shepard's house was a disaster. Well, perhaps not a disaster, but it was clear it was a bachelor's house and that he couldn't be bothered with housework. Dirty dishes were piled in the sink, a basket piled with dirty clothes was left in the hall and bits of newspapers were scattered over what sparse furniture he had. "Sorry about the mess," he offered again, but his voice was missing any sort of sincerity. He wasn't sorry at all, she realized. And more than ever she was certain that she could leave Alberta and go back home to Ontario with a clear conscience after today. Nell certainly did not belong here.

Along with the guilt came an intense wave of relief. Because while she'd felt all along that telling Callum about Nell was the *right* thing, it certainly wasn't the *easy* thing. Growing up without a father had affected Avery profoundly and she didn't want that for Nell. But telling Callum was risky, too. Crystal had named her guardian but a biological father could challenge that arrangement, couldn't he?

But Callum Shepard had no interest in being a father. That was as plain as the nose on her face. And Avery wanted to keep Nell with her for always. Setting the guidelines was the second reason she was here in Cadence Creek.

She perched on a corner of the couch, the only space free of papers or random clothing that hadn't been put away. With Nell tucked in the crook of her arm, she sat her purse on her knee and took out her wallet. "Here," she said, handing out the plastic-covered card. "This is her birth certificate."

He took the card from her fingers and looked at it a moment before handing it back. "That doesn't prove anything."

"You're listed as the father."

"She could have put anyone's name on there."

Indignation burned through Avery's veins and she fought to keep her voice down. "But she didn't put anyone's name. She put *yours*. And you know the dates add up. Crystal wouldn't lie about something like that." She shifted a little. Truth was, Crystal had been going to leave it blank. One of the last conversations they'd had was when Avery had finally convinced her to name Callum as the father on record.

He took a seat in a chair across from her and rested his elbows on his knees. "I beg your pardon because this is going to sound harsh, so let's just get it out of the way, shall we? Yes, I had a weekend fling with your sister. But it wasn't one-sided. She was just as willing as I was. And as far as her not lying about something like that, what makes you so sure? She certainly kept the existence of her baby a secret. A lie of omission is still a lie, you know. Why not lie on the birth certificate as well?"

Her mouth opened and closed a few times as she struggled to find the right words to respond.

"I know that probably makes you angry," he continued, "but there it is."

The baby started to squirm in her arms and Avery shifted Nell's weight, hoping to keep her quiet a little while longer. She'd done what she'd set out to do. She'd told him. She'd given him a chance. Nothing else was required to keep her conscience clean. "That's it, then?"

"Was there more you wanted from me? Child support, perhaps?"

The cool tone of his voice eradicated any hope of them dealing with this amicably. He thought she was a lying money grubber even though he hadn't put it in those exact terms. Her nostrils flared as the words of a crushing set-down trembled on her tongue. There was no point stirring up any more of a hornet's nest, not when she was close to having what she wanted. She held Nell closer. "There's nothing I want from you, Mr. Shepard. I just thought you deserved to know you had a daughter. I didn't agree with Crystal's stance to not tell you. Now that I have, I'll be on my way."

On her way. Like it was a short drive around the corner to go home. It hadn't been easy to find him and in the end someone she knew had broken a few rules as a personal favor to get his contact information. Avery had taken a week off work—unpaid—in order to fly out here because how did you deliver this sort of news by phone or in a letter?

On one hand she'd half hoped that Callum would own up to his responsibilities so they could come to an agreement. In her mind she'd worked up a whole proposal for how she would raise Nell as her own but promise Callum he could be involved in his daughter's upbringing. It had been quite inspired, actually, covering almost any contingency she could think of. The perfect plan so that Nell would have a loving home with her but would also grow up knowing her father—something Avery and Crystal had never had.

The speech was going to go to waste, but the end result was the same. Nell was going home with her. If Callum wasn't interested, that was his business. She would do everything to make sure Nell had a full, happy life.

She slid her purse strap over her shoulder and stood, tucking Nell's blanket closer around her. Nell's tiny dark eyes were open—at first they'd seemed blue but now Avery was sure they were going to be brown, like Callum's. Avery blinked against sudden tears and made her way out of the cluttered living room to the front door again.

"Wait."

Her hand was reaching for the knob when his voice stopped her. She turned around to find him standing in the space between the living room and kitchen, indecision marking his face.

"Why?" he asked quietly. "Why did you disagree with her about telling me?"

"Why do you think?"

He frowned. "If I really were the father, wouldn't Crystal have wanted to at least ask for financial support?"

Avery studied him. "She said you were very clear during your…brief time together, that as far as you were concerned weddings were all a sham and you never wanted to have either a wife or kids."

Whatever feeling she'd sensed behind the dark depths of his eyes was quickly shuttered away. "And you didn't agree with her?" he asked.

Did it really matter if he believed her? Perhaps it was better if he didn't. She could walk away free and clear without having to give up her daughter. That's what Nell was to her now. Avery had had her since birth and the love she had for her was so pure, so deep…

And that was why she knew she couldn't lie, even though telling the truth complicated everything and risked the very relationship she cherished most. When it came to Nell, Avery had to know that every decision she made was true and honest. When the time came for Avery to explain about Nell's parents, she wanted to have a clear conscience. No white lies, no glossing over of the truth. Avery had been brought up that way and it had sucked. If there was any way at all that Nell could know her father, Avery wanted to make that possible.

"Crystal and I grew up without a father," she explained quietly. "He took off when I was only eighteen months old—I have no memories of him. He left my mother pregnant with Crystal. We didn't have a bad life—I'm not saying that," she hurried to assure him, though it hadn't exactly been ideal either. "But to say I didn't wonder what it would have been like…that something wasn't missing…"

She met his gaze. He was watching her curiously and she realized that despite his radical change in appearance, the dark depths of his eyes were the same. Mysterious and magnetic all at once.

"Even the divorce kids in school spent time with their dads and I didn't even know where mine was or what he looked like," she explained. "I don't want Nell to have those same feelings because her mother wasn't strong enough to tell the truth when it mattered."

"You're not her mother."

The words were like a slap, and at that moment Avery knew he'd never understand. She rubbed her hand along Nell's back, feeling the warmth through the blanket. "Oh, yes, I am. In every possible way that counts."

She opened the door, feeling the warm July air puff against her face. The sun was just starting its descent and this side of the yard was awash with golden light. Nell twisted her head irritably, trying to get the glare out of her eyes.

Avery shifted her so that her small head was tucked safely into the curve of her neck and made her way down the steps.

"Miss Spencer."

She turned around. "What?"

He'd come outside in his stocking feet and stood at the top of the steps, hands on his hips. He really was intimidating looking with his scruffy beard and semi-wild hair and muscular build that Avery knew came from years of military training and now, apparently, manual labor.

Intimidating and manly and innately sexy all at the same time. That much hadn't changed, either. Avery clenched her teeth together. Like that really mattered.

"Where are you staying tonight?"

"I don't know." Truth be told, she'd come straight here from the airport, wanting to get the conversation over with first. She'd probably go back to Edmonton and find a room there. Was the town of Cadence Creek even big enough for a hotel?

"There's a bed-and-breakfast in town. That's probably the nicest. Otherwise there's a hotel out closer to the highway."

Avery held back a snort. His concern was so touching. Not like *he* was putting himself out and offering any hospitality. She got the feeling that Callum Shepard was in it for one person and one person only—himself, and anyone else be damned.

"Thanks," she answered, and turned her back on him.

It took a minute to get Nell buckled into her car seat and Avery could tell that the baby was growing more restless. They'd have to find a place to relax and soon, because Nell was going to need a diaper change and a bottle and some playtime.

Without saying another word to Callum she started the car and turned it around, heading back out the driveway.

When she looked in her rearview mirror, he was still standing on the steps, watching them leave.

CHAPTER TWO

AVERY HAD SURMISED that twenty-four hours might not be enough time to work things out with Callum, so when she'd booked her return flight she'd left a full day between arrival and departure. Since Callum wasn't at all interested in Nell, she called the airline and asked about switching to an earlier flight. Unfortunately, because it was high season, everything was sold out. She could put herself on the standby list, but traveling standby with a baby didn't sound like her favorite way to spend a day. They'd just make a mini vacation of it, then spend the full day in Cadence Creek and then head back as planned.

They stayed at the bed-and-breakfast and now, in the bright sun of a July morning, she had the window to their room open. A perfumed breeze wafted in from the flower gardens and Avery could hear birds singing in the bushes as they perched on the edge of the birdbath nestled among the plants. She'd enjoyed a full breakfast in the dining room and now Nell was buckled into her seat, staring at a bar of brightly colored toys.

Nell had been so good last night. They'd checked in and Avery had changed her, mixed up a bottle and fed her. Then they'd taken a bath together in the big tub and Avery had put her to bed in the portable playpen she'd brought as a second piece of luggage.

Traveling light wasn't an option with infants, but she wouldn't have it any other way. Despite the change in bed, Nell had only woken once in the night to be fed, and the bed-and-breakfast owners had moved a rocking chair into the room when they'd seen she had a baby. All in all it had been extremely comfortable.

"Come on, pumpkin. We've got a whole day to kill. Why don't we explore a little? There must be something to do in this town."

She'd had time to think about yesterday's events. While she was sad that Nell wasn't going to grow up knowing her father, the knowledge that Callum wasn't going to challenge her custody of Nell put a new spring in her step. She put a lace-trimmed bonnet on Nell's tiny head and once outside the bed-and-breakfast, she placed her in an umbrella stroller. They made their way through the small town, sticking to the few streets that had sidewalks and a selection of stores. It really was a cute little community with definite Western flair. False-fronted shops lined the streets and hanging flower baskets decorated the lampposts.

There was an old-fashioned general store that carried daily necessities as well as a selection of penny candy and knickknacks; a small department store dealing with household items and mostly work clothing and a hardware store. Farther along she found a craft shop that was charming, and they spent several minutes browsing inside. Avery knew she shouldn't, but she walked out with four balls of soft rose-colored yarn and a new pattern. She could tuck the yarn into the corners of her suitcase, and the pattern would knit up a sweet sweater and cap for Nell to wear when the weather turned chilly this fall. Avery looked down at the baby in the stroller and felt her heart swell. Autumn was her favorite time of year, and this year she and Nell would cozy up together during the longer evenings and she could knit to her heart's content.

They stopped at a bakery and Avery paid closer attention. This was her world—sugar and flour and butter and all the other mysterious, wonderful things that went into baking. The plain storefront window and shelving showcased a good selection of what she guessed to be high-quality items—good home-cooking if she were any judge. The bread was golden-brown and looked beautifully light, the pies were heavy with fruit, the crusts perfectly fluted and the meringue on the lemon ones stood a good two inches thick, the swirled peaks golden. There were cookies, squares, and cakes, too, but the cakes were boring: vanilla and chocolate, plainly decorated, without a bit of creativity. There was no fondant or sugar flowers, just buttercream piped through various tips. And only one lonely tray of chocolate cupcakes. Nice, but lacking in imagination and technique for sure.

She bought a cupcake and ventured back outside to eat it. Two stores away she spied a bench and she pushed the stroller to it, locked the wheels, handed Nell a rattle to keep her occupied and finally bit into the cake.

It wasn't bad. Not imaginative by any stretch, but the texture was good. A higher grade of cocoa would make a big difference. It wasn't quite to The Icing on Top standard, but then Avery made her living at the boutique bakery, specializing in cakes and cupcakes to order. She was always looking for new variations to experiment with, and loved how every day she always made something new. Lately her favorite had been making custom decorations for the tops of cupcakes. Her favorite so far had been the tiny mortarboards she'd done for June graduations, complete with gold leaf tassels. For one party she'd done red velvet cupcakes with white buttercream to match the red-

and-white school colors. They'd been a huge hit. And last month had been insane with weddings. More and more brides were choosing cupcakes over a traditional wedding cake. The lemon chiffon cakes with edible flowers on top were to die for.

She'd just licked the last of the frosting from her fingers when a shadow fell over the bench. She angled her face up to see Callum standing over them. At least this time his shirt was neatly tucked in and his hair had been combed...sort of. It still hung past his collar, giving him a rough and ready appearance, and he hadn't shaved, either. She usually didn't go in for facial hair, but she had to admit his rugged appearance made him seem both a little dangerous and incredibly sexy.

Her heart began to pound faster as she looked up into his eyes. Not because it was him, she assured herself, but because she hadn't planned on seeing him again and having him appear out of the blue felt like trouble was on its way. She should have known better than to let down her guard—should have known it had been too easy yesterday.

"Hello," she said quietly.

"Hi. I stopped by the bed-and-breakfast looking for you. Jim and Kathleen said you'd decided to have a look around town."

Her heartbeat quickened even more. "So you came looking for me?"

"Yeah. I did."

The sidewalk traffic was sparse and while Avery didn't want anyone eavesdropping on their conversation, there was a small comfort in being in a public place. "Do you want to sit down, Callum?"

She'd used his first name, she realized. Up until now it had been Mr. Shepard. Even this small familiarity seemed intimate and she made a point of breaking eye contact, looking down at Nell. She fussed with the baby's outfit even though everything was perfectly fine.

"You don't want to go somewhere more private?" he asked, and her pulse skipped.

"There's no one around, and Nell likes it outside. See how contented she is?"

Some "ba, ba" sounds came from the stroller, along with rattles from the toy as Nell batted her hands up and down.

The shadow disappeared as Callum moved to the side and took a seat on the bench.

Avery looked over at him. He was staring at Nell, his face unreadable. Like he was looking for something and not finding it. She waited a moment or two and then nudged. "Is there something you wanted to talk to me about?"

He sat back, resting his hands on his jeans. "About yesterday…"

"I believe you made your thoughts clear."

"I was shocked."

"Clearly." Nell dropped the rattle and Avery picked it up, dusted it off and gave it back to her.

"Wouldn't you be?" he asked quietly. "If someone showed up on your doorstep with news like that?"

"So you no longer think I'm a con artist out to scam you?"

"I never called you that."

She looked him square in the eye. "You thought it."

He looked away first this time. "Yes, I did."

Last night she'd had time to consider his response. Yes, he'd been rude and boorish but she put herself in his shoes and understood the skepticism. Then she'd spent too much time wondering at the change in him. The man she remembered had been friendly and fun, though at times he'd stood away from the others, looking lonely. But he'd been impeccably groomed with not a hair out of place, and he'd lit up when Crystal walked into a room…

"Look, Miss Spencer…Avery." He, too, dropped the formality and it did something funny to her insides, hearing him say her name like that.

He sighed. "Why did you come? What did you expect me to say?" He paused. "How did you really see all this playing out?"

"Which question do you want me to answer first?"

"Whatever explains it best," he replied.

She waited for a couple of ladies to pass by. They paused and smiled down at Nell—she really was an angel—before carrying on their way.

"I meant what I said about you having a right to know," she began, fighting to keep her voice even. "And Nell has a right to know about you, too. But I also meant what I said about not wanting anything from you. I didn't come here looking for money or…material support. Crystal gave me guardianship of Nell and we have a good home together. It's not big but it's comfortable and cozy. I love her as my own. I want to watch her grow up and when she's old enough I want to be able to tell her the truth about her parents."

"You mean like how she has a dad who couldn't be bothered with her?"

Avery's gaze snapped to him in surprise. Damn him, she still couldn't read his expression. Was he saying he believed Nell was his now? Or merely speaking in generalities? She took her time coming up with a response. After all, she didn't want to antagonize him. She was walking a precarious line.

"That would rather be up to you," she said softly. "But perhaps more accurate would be a dad who cared enough to see she was brought up in a home where she was wanted and loved."

"You want me to give up my rights."

She could feel his eyes on her, penetrating like they were boring a hole right into her skull. "Do I want to legally adopt her? Of course. This isn't about denying you anything, Callum. It's about a secure future for Nell." She made herself face him. "Just yesterday you were certain you didn't have any rights. Have you changed your mind?"

His eyes were dark and rich, like the deepest espresso she used in her mocha fudge recipe. They were the kind of eyes that a woman could get lost in if she let herself. The kind that held dark secrets. A man like Callum Shepard was a broody, wounded warrior that a lot of women would see as a personal challenge. The kind that would make a woman want to be the one to break down the walls and get to the man underneath.

Assuming, of course, they didn't get their hearts broken first. Avery certainly couldn't afford a challenge like that. That sort of thinking almost always ended in disaster. She'd seen way too many relationships fail because one of the people involved felt they could "fix" the other. She liked to think she was smarter than that.

"Her hair," he said softly, but the built-in roughness to his voice made it sound deep and husky and sent delicious tingles along the back of her neck.

"What about it?"

"It's dark and curly. Like mine."

Her lips dropped open. "Seriously? That's what convinced you? I'm a liar but the hair doesn't lie?"

The corner of his mouth twitched. "You're insulted. Not as much fun to be on the other side of judgment, Miss Spencer?"

Nell began to fuss, brilliant timing as it saved her from

answering. Avery made herself busy by unclipping the T-strap securing the baby and then lifted her out, put her on her knee and held her snugly while her free hand straightened the frilly dress, smoothing it over white bottoms that covered her diaper in a profusion of ruffles. Content to be cuddled, Nell shoved her fist in her mouth and gnawed on it happily.

"I'm going to suggest something and I don't want you to get offended again." Callum leaned back, resting against the bench.

"I can't promise that," she responded. "But let's hear it anyway."

"I'd like a paternity test."

The words made it sound all so real, which was ridiculous because Avery knew she wouldn't have come all this way if it weren't real to begin with. Last night she'd been angry but strangely relieved that he'd wanted nothing to do with Nell. How terrible did that make her? She was well aware that the feelings of relief were based on what was best for *her* and not best for Nell. She would have given anything to have known her father as she was growing up. How could she be relieved that Nell wouldn't have that, either? It was beyond selfish.

A paternity test would prove that Nell was his. Then how far would he push things? Would he demand custody? Parental rights, certainly…

"You still don't believe me," she answered shakily.

He sat up and leaned toward her a little. "Look, it's not personal. It wouldn't matter who was sitting here right now, I would still have my doubts. I would still want concrete proof. I don't take *anyone* at their word, okay? Words change. Proof? That doesn't change."

"And when you have that proof? What then?"

"I don't know. I'll cross that bridge when I come to it."

He could have the power to take Nell away. Avery had been well aware of it before she'd even set out on this trip. It was why she'd put it off for so long. She just hadn't been able to make herself do it, to plant the seeds of her own destruction. Because losing Nell *would* destroy her.

Nell was the only family Avery had left. Years ago she'd still had her mother, but Laura had moved to Vancouver and rarely ever contacted the two girls, she was so involved in her own life. They'd been abandoned not only by one parent, but by both. With Crystal gone, there was no one. Except Nell—Avery's reason for getting up in the morning—and usually several times during the night, too. Especially lately. "She's all I've got," she whispered.

Maybe she shouldn't have come. Maybe she should have just let it lie. Just her luck she had an overactive conscience.

"Relax," he said. "You saw my place. Do I look like the kind of guy prepared for full-time fatherhood? What would I do with a baby and a farm to run?"

He leaned forward, close enough that she could see the fine lines in the corners of his eyes, and how his dark brown irises had tiny flecks of gold close to the pupil.

"I have no intention of taking her away from you," he said with surprising gentleness. "If that's what's worrying you."

Tears pricked the back of her eyes and she blinked them away. "But you still want proof," she whispered hoarsely.

"I *need* proof."

"I fly back to Ontario tomorrow."

"Surely you can change your flight."

Of course she could. But it wasn't as easy as all that. "I do have a job, you know. I took a week off, but I have to be back…"

"A few days," he suggested. "Enough time to set up the test and have it done. You don't even have to stay and wait for the results. Once they're in, we can discuss things over the phone."

She looked down at Nell, whose attention was focused on a bright blue button. Her chubby fingers pulled and played with it, and Avery bounced her knee a little bit, making the baby look up and giggle with a toothless grin. She could afford a few days but that was all. When she wasn't working she wasn't earning money, and there were two of them to support now.

Besides, she didn't want to play difficult. It was a simple and logical request considering the circumstances. If she refused, he could get nasty about it and have a court-ordered test if he wanted to, because whether or not he wanted to be a dad, for some reason he really wanted to know definitively one way or the other.

"A few days, but that's all. We can stay here at the B&B. I'll leave the arrangements for the test up to you, though. I've never done this before. I'm guessing you'll have to contact your local doctor and set something up."

"It's not something I have experience in, either," he pointed out. "But I'll look after it. Give me your cell number so I can call you about the arrangements."

She reached into her purse and took out a business card, flipped it over and wrote her number on the back. Nell grabbed at the pen, but Avery diverted her hand and reached into the diaper bag at her feet instead, and pulled out a teething ring. "Here, sweet pea. This is better for you to chew on than a pen."

She gave him the card and he flipped it over. "The Icing on Top?" he asked.

"I'm a baker," she replied. "I decorate cakes. Mostly cupcakes."

"Cupcakes," he repeated, making it sound as if it were the silliest job in the world.

Despite the improved tone to today's meeting, it was clear to Avery that Callum had very little respect for her. It began with his skeptical attitude and continued with the assumption she could simply change her schedule to suit him and the dismissive tone when he asked about her job. She needed to be careful not to antagonize him, but she wasn't going to go along with absolutely everything just because he suggested it.

She checked her watch. It was getting close to noon, and well-behaved as she was, Nell was going to start getting hungry soon. Avery knew from experience that leaving it too long would send the baby into full-on meltdown. "Is there a restaurant nearby? Somewhere that we can sit down, where they'd heat a bottle for me?"

He shrugged. "The Wagon Wheel diner is around the corner. It's a run-of-the-mill family place, but the food's good."

"She's going to be hungry soon. I'd rather stay a step ahead than deal with a cranky baby." Politeness seemed to demand that she ask. "Would you care to join us, Callum?"

He stepped back. "Thanks, but I don't think so. I like to keep to myself. And showing up with you and the baby... This is a small town. The gossip mill would be running before we'd even ordered."

The rebuff felt like a slap. He couldn't even call Nell by her name, instead referring to her as "the baby." And he didn't want to be seen in public with Avery—not for this conversation and certainly not sharing a meal. She shoved the pen and teething ring into her purse and made short work of strapping Nell back into the stroller. She stood and put her hands on the handles. "We won't keep you, then."

"Yes, I need to get back. Work to be done."

His precious work. Of course.

"Call me when you have an appointment time." She

lifted her chin. "If you could do that right away, I'd appreciate it. I do have to adjust my travel plans."

"Yes, ma'am."

He turned and walked away from her. She watched him go, the way his long stride ate up the ground and the pockets of his faded jeans shifted with the movement.

The man she remembered from the wedding had been tall and smiling, purposeful but with an easiness about him—like he might actually know how to let loose and have fun. What had happened to cause such a difference in him in such a short time? Because this version of Callum Shepard was abrasive, grouchy and had a very large stick up his posterior.

Except there'd been the gentle way he'd said he didn't want to take Nell away from her. Like he understood.

And the way he insisted on proof as if he'd been lied to before.

Nell started to cry and Avery turned away from the sight of Callum walking away. Callum's reasons didn't matter. She'd go through the formality of a test for his peace of mind and then she'd go back to Ontario and get on with raising Nell.

The movement of the stroller on the sidewalk temporarily soothed the baby as they headed in the direction of the diner. She had to remember one important fact when it came to Callum. He'd had a fling with her sister when they'd barely known each other. And never, in either of their meetings, had he asked what had happened to Crystal, how she'd died.

What kind of guy did that?

She didn't like the answer.

CHAPTER THREE

CALLUM HUNG UP the phone and sat at the kitchen table for a moment, trying to make sense of his thoughts. Avery hadn't answered her cell, so he'd left a voice mail giving her the time of the doctor's appointment. It would take a day or two to get the test in, so he hadn't been able to get an appointment until midmorning on Friday. Avery probably wasn't going to be happy about that, but it was out of his hands.

If she could just understand his reasons for asking for it in the first place...

But she didn't nor would she. There was no sense bringing up the past when it couldn't be changed. He'd learned his lesson and was smart enough not to get caught in the same trap ever again.

Now he'd lost the better part of the day. He'd planned to put the cows in the west pasture until milking time and it hadn't happened. Then there was the load of hay he'd bought from the Diamond brothers over at Diamondback Ranch. It needed picking up.

Not to mention the fact that he ignored the house most of the time. He'd put on his last pair of jeans this morning and had thrown a load of laundry in the machine out of pure necessity. He knew the place looked bad. It hadn't taken Avery's turned-up nose yesterday to tell him that.

He'd probably been foolish to buy this place. He should have taken a job instead of trying to run everything solo. It was just…the idea of taking orders from someone again was so repulsive that he couldn't see himself doing it. And he'd chosen the farm because the most uncomplicated time in his life for as far back as he could remember had been working summers on his uncle's farm on the lower mainland. Nothing had been complicated when he'd been cutting hay or feeding calves or laughing—a lot.

It was the laughter he missed the most.

He knew everyone in Cadence Creek thought he was plumb crazy for wanting to raise dairy cows in the heart of beef country. Maybe he was. But for him the only real cow was a Holstein, and it made him happy. Five o'clock in the morning came early, but the time he spent in the milking parlor with the radio on was the best part of his day. Calm, quiet. Just him, the cows and country music.

And when George Grant had decided to retire and sell off his quota, it had seemed like the perfect opportunity.

Callum pushed away from the table and took his plate to the sink. It was full with dirty dishes. God, what a disaster. He had to do something, especially if Avery Spencer came around again.

He picked up the phone and dialed the only person he'd trusted since moving to the area: Tyson Diamond. Ty and his brother Sam ran the biggest ranch around but you'd never know it. Friendly, down-to-earth and always ready to offer advice or a willing hand, the brothers had eased Callum's way as he'd taken over Grant's farm. And neither of them had asked too many questions, either.

Ty answered on the first ring. "Tyson Diamond."

"Ty, it's Callum."

"Hey, brother." Callum suppressed a smile; Ty had an easy-going way about him that his older brother, Sam, didn't and it showed, even in the simple greeting. There was a scuffling noise and then the sound cleared. "What can I do for you?"

"I need your advice. Or maybe your wife's advice."

"Clara? She's up at the house. I can get her to call you. What's it about?"

"I need a hand and thought she could recommend someone." He closed his eyes and shook his head. "I need someone to help me clean out this pigsty. I can't afford anyone really expensive…"

Ty's laugh came over the line. "You're calling for a maid."

"Just temporarily. To help me get caught up."

"You should talk to Angela. She might have someone at the women's shelter who's looking for a job or even just a few extra hours somewhere. If that'd be okay, I'll pass the info along."

"That'd be fine. And the sooner the better."

"Any particular reason?"

He thought of Avery looking down her nose at the state of his living room, then pictured her clear blue eyes as they'd stared into his this morning. "Uh, not really. Just needs to be done, and I don't have the time to do it."

"Nothing to do with the woman you were seen with in town this morning, then?"

This was exactly why he'd wanted to talk privately instead of on a bench in the middle of Main Street. "Honestly, you're a worse gossip than the women."

Ty's laugh echoed in his ear. "No gossip. I passed you on my way to the hardware store, but you were talking and didn't notice. But you're awfully sensitive about it…"

The teasing note in Ty's voice reminded Callum of what it was like to have friends, and the thought sent a spear of pain through him. "If you could pass on the request, that'd be great."

"Yeah, yeah, sure. No problem. Got that load of hay for you here, too, whenever you're ready. We can deliver it on the weekend if you like."

"Thanks, that'd be great. Gotta run."

He hung up and wiped his hand over his face. Tyson reminded him of Pete, and maybe a little of Matt and the others. Always good for a laugh or a favor.

Except they weren't anymore. Callum's fingers tightened on the edge of the table. They'd all followed their orders—all except Callum. He'd been sleeping off a night of drunkenness in the brig. Because of it, the section had gone out without him. When the IED went off, he'd been safe and sound. They hadn't, and he'd had to live with that ever since.

On Friday morning Avery splurged on a long-distance call to her boss, Denise. Working at The Icing On Top was a dream job, and she wanted to reassure Denise that she'd be back to work as planned in a few days. Denise had been incredibly sympathetic to Avery's situation, giving her whatever time she needed after Crystal's death. Instead of applying for parental leave and trying to make do on a reduced salary, Denise had even allowed Avery to bring Nell to work at the bakery. Once Nell was older, Avery knew she would have to put her in day care, but for now, during these first precious months, Avery was able to keep Nell with her. She was getting quite good at decorating with the baby in the Snugli carrier, and she kept the playpen in the back office and a baby monitor in the bakery kitchen. When the time came for Denise to expand, Avery wanted to be first in line to manage the new location.

She owed Denise a lot, and the last thing she wanted to

do was take her generosity for granted. She wanted to re-assure Denise that she'd be back to work first thing after her return.

Denise's voice sounded stressed on the other end of the line as she finally answered on the sixth ring. "Hey, I was going to call you today," she said.

"Is something wrong?"

"Not wrong, per se. Just…you don't have to hurry back this week after all. The bakery's going to be closed for a few weeks for repairs."

"Repairs? What happened?" Avery sat heavily on the bed as she counted the missed wages in her mind.

"A fire at the pizza place next door. We're okay—just some damage to the front awning which is easily replaced. But the electrics are a mess and there's a fair bit of water damage. There's no way we can reopen until that's taken care of."

"Oh, Denise. I'm so sorry." She knew what having to close would do to a bottom line.

"I know. But that's what insurance is for." Denise paused. "How are things going, anyway?"

"I really don't know." Avery sighed. "Callum is very different from the guy I remember, and he's not too keen on Nell. I haven't seen him in a couple of days. We're going for a paternity test in a few minutes."

"Well, that's sort of what you wanted, right? Full custody without a bunch of drama?" Denise's voice was hopeful. God bless her, Denise always tried to look on the bright side.

Avery shrugged even though Denise wasn't there to see her. "I don't really know what I want. I want Nell to know her father like I never did, but I want to have her all to my-self, too. Trying to figure out how to have it both ways is proving a challenge."

"Well, if anyone can do it, you can. You remember that. You're way stronger than you think. Not everyone could have stepped in and done what you've done the last few months. Keep your chin up and I'll be in touch when I know more about a reopening date."

"Will do. And thanks," she added warmly. "For everything."

"I know, I know. Boss of the year."

Avery could picture Denise's crooked smile. "Decade. Century, even."

After they hung up Avery let out a big breath. She was still trying to process the news when Callum's truck pulled up outside the bed-and-breakfast. Nerves churned in Avery's tummy. She hurried to grab the carrier and diaper bag so he didn't have to wait. When he met them on the walkway below the veranda, he hesitated only for a moment before turning and heading back to where his vehicle was parked.

Still avoiding any eye or physical contact, then. She didn't know why they were both so tense. It was just a swab test. No results would be had for at least a week. And she was in no doubt of the results, after all. Crystal might have kept secrets, but she wouldn't have lied to Avery about that.

Avery carried the car seat to the waiting vehicle, a crew cab half-ton built for function but without a lot of bells and whistles. Once the belt was fastened securely, she stepped up into the front seat. "This thing is huge."

"It does the job," he replied, starting the engine. Avery felt weird sitting there with him, enclosed in the cab with no escape, with the scent of his aftershave filling the air. It was just her dumb luck that she'd thought him handsome from the beginning. It made her feel awkward, and she hoped he didn't pick up on it. How embarrassing.

Thankfully it only took a few minutes to get to the

small, neat building that housed the doctor's office. Callum hopped out and then came around the truck and opened her door before she even got the diaper bag over her shoulder.

He let her carry the car seat with Nell in it. She bit down on her lip. To her recollection, he'd never called Nell by name, always referring to her as "the baby."

And not once had he touched her or bothered to pick her up.

Today, Avery realized as she stepped through the door he held open, was truly a formality. Because Callum was definitely no father.

Callum's heart wouldn't settle down from the weird pattering that pressed against his chest. This was stupid. It was a simple test. A mouth swab and it was all over. Results in a few days that would prove...

He clenched his jaw as Avery passed by him, her light floral scent teasing his nostrils. He didn't seem to remember her being this headstrong. She'd been a bit of a wallflower at the wedding. But the woman with him today was tough and determined. And beautiful. Her skin practically glowed and he noticed a few freckles dotting her nose, making her seem younger than he knew she must be. And when she smiled at the receptionist and announced their arrival, he caught his breath.

Her hair was back in a ponytail, but a few pale strands had come loose and framed her face. She looked pretty in a natural sort of way. So unlike her sister, who'd been fond of bright colors and painted nails and flawless makeup. There wasn't a man alive who wouldn't have had his head turned by Crystal Spencer. She was a knockout.

Past tense, he reminded himself as he stood beside Avery. And Avery was as different from her sister as night and day. Oh, there was a resemblance he could see now, in the tilt of her nose and the shape of her eyes. But there was something different about her, something easier. Simpler. Crystal had been a bombshell, but Avery was the girl next door.

In her own very natural way, Avery Spencer was stunning.

He was still reeling from that realization when they sat to wait in the quiet waiting room. Callum closed his eyes briefly. Confidentiality be damned; before the day was out people would know he'd been here with a woman and a baby. Even if they knew nothing about the paternity test, assumptions would start. Things had a way of spreading through a small town like wildfire.

He looked over at Nell, who was sitting on Avery's lap happily shaking a rattle shaped like a giraffe. His throat tightened. Deep down he knew what today's test was going to say. He had seen it first in the hair, but then he'd dug out an old family picture. His first impressions were correct. The resemblance was there, especially to his little sister, Taylor.

Nell was a Shepard through and through. His daughter. The very thought was enough to send his stomach plummeting to his feet. What on earth was he going to do with a kid?

This whole thing opened up too many old wounds. He couldn't stop thinking about Jane and the baby she'd had. Not to mention the fact that she'd lied so easily to his face for weeks before breaking his heart.

Dr. Lazowski called them in and the three of them entered the exam room together. No questions asked, just the quick procedure and they were done. "I'll send this off to the lab immediately," he said, writing in a chart. "And the results?"

"To my mailing address," Callum said tightly.

"And to mine." Avery stepped forward and gave him her address in Ontario. Suddenly Callum realized that this meant she was really leaving. And taking Nell with her. Just like that it was done. He wasn't even used to the idea of them being around and they would be out of his life.

"Thanks, Dr. Lazowski," Callum said, and they were back out in the waiting room again. It almost seemed like it had never happened. Nothing felt different, except knowing that now it was over, Avery and Nell would be flying back home in a few hours to wait for the results.

What was he going to do when they came back positive? Because he was sure they were going to. He'd been trying to come to grips with it over the last few days. He had a daughter. A child—something he'd never thought would happen. Not after everything in his past. Not after Jane and definitely not after what had happened overseas.

They got back in the truck and Callum paused. "Did you want to grab some lunch?"

Avery shook her head. "Our flight leaves in a few hours, and I have to take my rental car back. I'll just get something at the airport."

He deserved that; he'd turned down her offer the other day, after all. "That's fine, then."

He refused to look at her, or over his shoulder at Nell. It was probably just as well. Even if Nell was his—which he was now very certain she was—he had no business trying to be a full-time father. She belonged with Avery. And Avery's life was across the country, in her trendy apartment working in her trendy bakery while his whole savings—and a sizable loan—sat right here on his farm.

She insisted she didn't want financial support and he wasn't making a lot of money, but he would help out. It would be bad enough being an absentee dad, but no one was going to accuse him of being a deadbeat.

It was the very least his conscience demanded. So why did he feel like he was taking the easy way out?

Back at the inn he'd barely shut off the ignition when she was out of the truck and opening the side door to get Nell. She'd clearly planned ahead because she went inside and came right back out rolling her suitcase and carrying the packed-up playpen. The umbrella stroller was snapped up and stowed in the trunk of her car in no time flat and there was nothing more to do than say goodbye.

It was not how he'd envisioned this morning going. Not with her so…cold. He didn't quite know what he'd done to set her off, but she wouldn't even look him in the eye.

She turned to face him and pasted on a smile so fake it looked plastic. "I'll be in touch after we get the results."

"Right. You've got everything?"

"Yes."

"You don't need…" He didn't know how to finish the question. What was he trying to ask? Why was this so hard? He should be relieved that things were going back to normal, so why was he drawing the moment out rather than just opening the damn door for her?

"I don't need anything from you, Callum."

Well. That was clear, and a common enough refrain when all was said and done. Feeling helpless, he reached down and opened her car door, watched as she buckled Nell's seat into place. He swallowed, staring down at the tiny face with the innocently blinking eyes. He slid his gaze to Avery, who refused to look at him but slid behind the wheel. When he hesitated shutting the door, she finally looked up.

"It's time to go," she said, a tad bit impatiently. The tone rode on his nerves.

"Did I do something this morning? Something to make you rush off like this?" He didn't like leaving things on a sour note. Not when they were going to have to stay in touch for…

For years to come. *Years.* They would always be connected by Nell.

"Not at all," she answered. "This morning just reminded me of our positions in this whole thing. There's simply no sense prolonging things, don't you agree?"

No, dammit, he didn't agree, but couldn't say so without getting in over his head.

"Drive carefully," he said finally, and shut the door while she started the engine.

He watched her car go out the driveway and turn onto the dirt lane that connected to the paved road. It felt wrong watching her drive away like that, but what else was he supposed to do? She wanted nothing to do with him. Oh, perhaps she'd been curious, just like him. He hadn't imagined the way her eyes had snapped to his now and again, or the color that rose in her cheeks when he was around. She'd blushed that morning on the park bench.

But a little curiosity was a far cry from working together to raise a kid, wasn't it?

If she'd wanted full custody, she could have just let things stand and he never would have known the difference. Instead she'd come to find him, determined that he— and her niece—deserved to know each other.

He had to admire that. Except Miss Spencer gave him the impression that she always did the right thing, and that was a damned hard example for a flawed human being to follow.

Restless, he turned back to his truck and noticed the back door wasn't quite latched. He went to close it and when he looked in the window he saw the small stuffed giraffe. He reached in and picked it up. The fabric was soft and it made a jingling nose as he turned it over in his hand.

The scent of baby powder and soap still clung to the interior of the truck.

His kid. And he hadn't even held her in his arms, not once. He recalled Jane's voice explaining why she couldn't go through with the wedding. That the baby she carried wasn't really his; that she couldn't marry a man who would never be there for their family. And he heard his own voice, explaining in no uncertain terms to Crystal last spring that he wasn't interested in a wife and kids, when the truth was a family of his own had been all he wanted until Jane walked away, taking his dreams with her.

And then he'd gotten Crystal pregnant. And now, when faced with his biggest mistake, he was the one walking away. Perhaps Avery was the one driving, but he'd done nothing to stop her.

What kind of man was he?

An idiot, that's what.

Before he could change his mind, he shoved the giraffe in his pocket and hopped up into the cab of his truck to go after her.

CHAPTER FOUR

AVERY PULLED INTO the service station to fill up the rental before taking it back. For the past fifteen minutes of the drive, Nell had been crying. In her haste to leave Cadence Creek, Avery hadn't given her a bottle or changed her diaper.

She'd been too focused on getting away from Callum. The cold stranger who was so intent on *not* being a father that he insisted on a stupid paternity test when all the evidence he needed was right before his eyes.

She'd nearly forgotten that until this morning at the doctor's office when it had been a quick swab and back out on the street.

Nell's cries echoed through the closed window and Avery was embarrassed to find tears pricking behind her own lids, hot and humiliated. She clicked off the pump and printed out the receipt. She was just tucking it into her purse when a huge truck pulled in behind her and Callum jumped out.

Why did he have to be so dangerously good-looking? Right now he was walking toward her with long strides and his gaze was fixed on her face.

"Callum?"

He stood before her and she watched him swallow. Then

he reached into his pocket and pulled out Nell's tiny stuffed giraffe.

"You left this in my truck."

She reached out and took it, confused. "It's a giraffe. You followed me all the way to Edmonton to give me a five-dollar toy?"

He shoved his hands in his pockets. "I, uh…" He faltered and she looked up into his face. He was trying hard to keep from showing any emotion, any clue to his feelings, but she could tell it was costing him. A horn beeped; people were waiting to gas up and they were blocking the pumps.

"Can you pull into the parking area? Just give me five minutes. Please, Avery."

He said "please." And despite his best intentions she could see something on his face. Anxiety. Regret. She nodded briefly. "Just a few minutes. Sometimes it takes a while to get through security with baby gear."

She pulled over into the parking area and he followed, parking his truck beside her compact.

He met her by the back of her vehicle, and for a few seconds he didn't speak.

"You didn't follow me here to give me back a stuffed animal, did you?"

He shook his head. Avery's pulse started to thump. What did he want? And why on earth should she feel excited? Ten minutes ago she'd been angry, on her way home with a clear conscience. It was simpler this way. So why had she felt so very glad to see him striding across the pavement?

"She's mine," he blurted out.

That was not what Avery had expected. "I beg your pardon?"

His face softened. "She looks exactly like my baby sister did at that age. Today's appointment…it's a formality, Avery. I know she's mine. I've known it deep down for a few days now."

Avery's thoughts jumbled together. He had a sister? Callum was so gruff and solitary it seemed impossible to think of him surrounded by parents and siblings. And yet she knew he hadn't just hatched, fully formed, into the broody recluse he seemed to be.

And then there was the heady fact that without proof he was actually acknowledging that Nell was his daughter.

She was happy about that. And scared as hell, too. The same feelings she'd had that first day came rushing back. Afraid of what he might demand. Afraid of losing the most precious thing in her life.

"What changed your mind?"

He sighed. "It's a long story."

"I have time."

"Not if you have a plane to catch." He took a small step closer. "Do you absolutely have to go today?"

What on earth was he asking? Avery took a deep breath, trying to sort out her thoughts and remain rational. "I've already rescheduled my flight once."

"I know. And I know you have a job, but don't you have a little more vacation? Just to give me a chance to…"

He turned his head and looked through the back window at the car seat.

"A chance to what, Callum?"

He turned back and met her gaze. She felt the eye contact right to her toes. Yes, he looked rough and dangerous. He also looked uncertain, a little bit vulnerable, and sexy to boot. It made him hard to resist—not that she'd ever admit that to his face.

"A chance to get to know Nell a bit before you take her back with you," he answered.

For the first time he'd referred to her as Nell and not "the baby." That tiny detail went a long way to softening her to his plea.

"I'll make up whatever you'll lose in wages," he offered. "Just a little more time is all I'm asking."

She could take him up on his offer and that would solve her immediate money problem. Just her bad luck that she was scrupulously honest, then. "I'm already out wages anyway," she confessed. "I talked to my boss this morning. We're closed for a few weeks for repairs."

"So you *could* stay if you wanted to."

"Callum, I…" She wanted to say no. Wanted to go back to her apartment in Burlington and get back to a regular schedule. Surrounded by familiar things. But how could she deny him this little bit of time? How could she deny it to Nell? Oh, sure, she knew the baby wouldn't remember a thing. But over the years—if Callum stood up and took responsibility—Avery would be the one facilitating their time together.

Why not start it right now and set the tone for future dealings?

She swallowed. This was the beginning, then. From here on out she would be a part of Callum's life. Even if it was on the sidelines, they were inextricably connected.

Connected through something so precious and important it didn't really matter about her misgivings, did it? It had to be about what was best for Nell. Always.

"Please," he repeated again. "Just for a week or two. Then I promise I won't stand in your way. I know you have your own life to live."

She closed her eyes for a second. She had to be crazy to agree to such a thing. And then the words came tumbling out anyway.

"Okay. But first I really do need to take this car back.

Will you follow me and then we can drive back to Cadence Creek with you?"

"Of course."

His shoulders relaxed and Avery realized how tense he'd been, waiting for her answer. She couldn't believe she was doing this.

She went to go around the bumper of the car but Callum's hand reached out, catching her forearm. It was strong and warm and a little rough, and the proprietary contact sent electricity shooting through her limbs. She looked up into his eyes and nearly lost herself in the complicated depths. How was she ever going to get through two weeks under the same roof with him, if a single touch caused such a reaction within her?

"Thank you," he said softly. "I know you've turned your life upside down for this. Hell, you've been doing that for months now. I do appreciate it. More than you can imagine."

"It's what's best for Nell," she replied, her breath catching in her throat. "Follow me up to the rental car area, okay?"

She got behind the wheel and let out a long, slow breath.

She could do this for two weeks. It *was* for Nell. And yes, for Callum, too.

And she'd just keep her unexpected personal feelings out of it. They'd only complicate an already complicated situation.

The last thing she needed was to embarrass herself by developing a crush and make things awkward between them for the rest of her life.

Avery looked at the house with new eyes as they drove into the farmyard. It was nothing special. It had potential but

Callum had naturally been far too busy with farmwork to worry about the aesthetics of the property.

And yet there was something calm about it, and settled. In some ways it reminded Avery of the house they'd lived in when she was in first grade...or was it second? Mom had had a job in St. Catharines and she'd rented them a little house on a side street. A plain bungalow with a weeping willow out front.

She and Crystal had had skipping contests in the driveway, and had come in at night with red marks crisscrossing their legs from the jump ropes. It had been an easier time. Simpler, and unrushed. Funny how she should think about that now when she hadn't in years.

Callum parked the truck. "I'll help you take your things in," he said quietly. "I know you didn't pack for an extended stay, so if you want to wash anything, feel free to use the washer and dryer."

"Thanks." Truthfully Avery had wondered how she was going to get through two weeks with the few outfits she'd brought. Everything in her case was dirty and her nicer traveling clothes weren't really suited for around here.

"I've got to get started on chores soon. I know I said I wanted to spend time with her..."

Avery turned in her seat. "Callum, I know you have a farm to run and you can't drop everything and pretend it doesn't exist. I even understand that milking happens at the same time each day. There'll be time after that."

He looked relieved. "Okay, good."

"Let's just get inside, okay?"

"Right."

She stepped over the threshold and blinked. The place was transformed. There wasn't a thing out of place and it looked like it had been freshly dusted and vacuumed.

"You, uh…" She looked around and then back up into his eyes. "You really went at this place."

"I can't take the credit. It needed attention and I hired someone to come out and make it presentable."

"I see."

Awkward silence surrounded them. So far the only conversations they'd had had been regarding Nell, short and to the point. It was far different entering his house as a guest. How were they going to get through the next several days if things were so uncomfortable between them?

"Why don't I show you to the spare room?" Callum suggested. "I've got to go out to do the chores soon, but there's dinner in the Crock-Pot for later."

Dinner in the Crock-Pot? If she didn't know better, she'd think she was in the wrong house. "That'd be great."

He stepped ahead, presumably to lead her down the hall to her room. She stepped at the same time and they nearly collided. Callum instinctively reached out and steadied her with his hands. His fingers were warm on her skin and her throat seemed suddenly tight as her gaze darted to his for just a moment. His chest was only a few inches away from hers and as she stared at him, a muscle ticked in his jaw.

She looked away and he stepped back, dropping his hands, but the damage had been done. He'd touched her, and shockingly enough her body had responded in a wholly feminine way.

He cleared his throat and made his way down the hall, stopping in front of a door. When he opened it, she was met with a plain but comfortable enough looking room. The mint-green walls were a little bright for the small space, and the beige carpet was rather dull. The bed was old but the bedding was clean—including the floral spread that probably dated back to the eighties.

"It's not exactly the Ritz," he said quietly.

"It's fine," she assured him. "It's got a bed and room for me to set up Nell's playpen." She put the diaper bag on the bed and the carrier on the floor. Within a few seconds she had the baby unfastened and on her arm again. It seemed odd that she suddenly thought of Nell as protection. Callum looked so uneasy that she forced a bright smile. "It's perfect, Callum, thank you."

His face eased and his gaze shifted to Nell. The frilly bonnet covered the fringe of dark hair and as he looked at them Nell popped her thumb into her mouth and curled into the curve of Avery's neck, peeking out at him from beneath her lashes. For a second she thought she glimpsed tenderness on his features, which was suddenly replaced by pain. Her heart seized a little. Was he thinking about Crystal? Or something else?

Then he schooled his face again and the moment was gone. "Right. Well. Do you need help bringing in your things?"

"I'd appreciate that, Callum. I'm used to managing with one good arm and a baby on the other, but it's nice to have an extra set of hands once in a while."

"I'll be right back."

While he was gone she took a minute to change Nell's diaper. As she usually did, she talked to the baby in a light, singsongy voice, loving how Nell gazed up at her and then gave a bubbly laugh as Avery made nonsensical sounds. Within seconds Avery rolled up the sides of the soiled diaper and fastened it with the tape, slid a fresh one beneath Nell's bottom, secured it snugly, replaced her frilly pants and had her on her arm.

She turned around and caught him watching from the doorway, her suitcase and the playpen at his feet.

"Oh, you're back." Her cheeks heated again. How long had he been standing there?

He cleared his throat. "You want everything in here?"

"That would be lovely, thanks. Could you point me in the direction of the bathroom? I'd like to wash my hands."

"Oh, of course." He put the gear down quickly and led the way to the bathroom that was just across the hall from his room. "Just make yourself at home," he said. "I've got to get out to the barns."

She turned on the taps and he watched for a moment, unsure of what to say. In the end he said nothing at all.

Instead he went out to the barn to get started on the chores and the milking and Avery prepared a bottle and got ready to put Nell down for an afternoon nap.

Avery wasn't sure how long Callum would be in the barn, so she let supper simmer in the Crock-Pot and did a load of laundry while Nell slept. After the baby woke, she spread out Nell's activity mat, determined that the baby should have some tummy time as the parenting books recommended. Besides, Nell was nearly rolling over now. Avery smiled and touched the downy-soft hair on Nell's head. She was enjoying celebrating every milestone.

When the baby was truly dissatisfied at being on her stomach, Avery put her on her back and grabbed a brightly colored stuffed animal, playing with her and making funny noises until Nell giggled, the big belly laughs making a smile spread across Avery's face.

That was how Callum found them when he came inside, smelling strongly of cows and a hint of straw.

She hopped up right away. Things were so awkward that she wanted to break the ice somehow. "We thought we'd have some playtime before dinner."

"You waited?"

He sounded surprised. It was well after seven.

"When I'm working, it's usually later than this by the time we get home and I get her fed and make something for myself. I thought…well, I thought maybe we could eat together."

And probably struggle for things to say. Clearly Callum wasn't a talker. Which was strange, because she remembered him as being a lot more sociable at the wedding. They'd done a group trip on the *Maid of the Mist* to see the falls and he'd been joking around just fine, especially when the boat had turned around and the water from the roaring falls had drenched them all despite the thin blue ponchos provided.

The rehearsal dinner had been at a winery about an hour from the falls, very intimate and he'd had no problem sliding his chair closer to Crystal's as they'd chatted in low voices. He'd worn black trousers and a dress shirt open at the collar, she remembered.

She blinked. Seriously, it was like looking at two totally different men.

"Let me get cleaned up first," he suggested. "I smell like the barn."

She got the feeling that smelling like the barn wasn't as big an issue when he was here alone.

"Nell's nearly ready for bed. I'll give her a bottle while you're doing that. It's always nice to be able to eat without dealing with a screaming baby."

She fed Nell on the sofa and when the bottle was half gone, Nell's lashes started to droop. A minute more and her lips went slack, a dribble of the formula running out of the corner of her mouth. Avery wiped it gently and put the baby on her shoulder, rubbing her back. Half awake, the baby let out a burp and then within moments, relaxed in Avery's arms.

This was her favorite time of the day—when the pace slowed down and Nell fell asleep in her arms. That was when she knew everything was just as it was meant to be. That it would all be okay.

She tucked Nell into the playpen, covered her with the blanket and tiptoed out of the room.

She found Callum in the kitchen, mixing something in a pot on the stove. He was frowning and she stepped forward. "Anything I can help with?"

"The lady who was here this morning left instructions on how to thicken this, but it's all lumpy."

Avery smiled. "You have to whisk it in. Do you have a whisk?"

"Probably not."

She grinned. "A strainer, then? I can stir out as many lumps as I can, but we'll have to strain it."

He found one in the back of the cupboard and brought it out.

While she tried to repair the damage he put the vegetables in a bowl and sliced the beef onto a platter. Once the table was set she strained the gravy into a bowl. "I take it you don't cook much," she observed.

"Not really."

"Then what do you eat?" She flushed a little. "I don't mean that the way it sounded."

He shrugged. "I can manage to fry a steak or pork chop and bake a potato."

It sounded terribly boring. They sat down together in the silence.

"Are you as uncomfortable as I am?" she finally asked, putting her hands on her lap.

His gaze snapped up and met hers. "Should I be?"

She couldn't help the smile on her face. At least it wasn't just her. "Oh, you're back to answering a question with a question. So you *do* find this awkward."

"It's a heck of a situation," he admitted.

The scent of his soap mingled with the rich scent of beef and potatoes. His hair was wet from his shower and his T-shirt showed off a workingman's physique. She hardly knew him and she was in his house. Sharing a meal. Sleeping in a bed.

Heck of a situation indeed.

He passed her the bowl of vegetables first. "Here, help yourself," he suggested, and for a few minutes the sounds of forks and spoons scraping on plates was all that was heard.

Avery took a bite of beef. It was delicious, but now she was ultra-aware of chewing and wondering if he could possibly hear it.

She put down her fork. "I don't know how to do this," she admitted. "To act…normal. It feels like a first date sort of thing only without the, well, *date*. And I don't go on many of those…"

"Since Nell?"

She toyed with a piece of carrot on her plate, pushing it around with her fork. "Even before Nell," she admitted quietly. "I'm kind of shy, really."

And for a long time she'd been content to be in Crystal's shadow. No one demanded anything of her there.

"Oh," he answered. Then he gave a sideways smile, just a hint but enough that it sent something strange swirling through her tummy. "I'm not much of a social butterfly, either."

"It wasn't always that way, though, was it?" Maybe she'd only known him for a weekend, but he'd been very outgoing, laughed a lot. It just went to show how erroneous first impressions could be.

He shrugged. "Things change. People change. They grow up."

Avery blinked. She wasn't sure how to reply to that.

They ate for a bit and then she couldn't help it; she had to ask.

She put down her fork. "Did something happen that made you grow up?"

The air in the room grew very still, like a warning.

"Never mind," she said quickly, picking up her fork again. "I don't mean to pry. I mean...we hardly know each other."

"No, you're right. I'm very different from the guy you met a year ago. Truth is, that wedding weekend was mostly an act. I was trying to forget something and I used your sister to do it. So, yeah. Something happened."

Oh, the questions that made her want to ask! Forget what happened—she was more interested in *who* had happened to him and what damage they'd done. And what had gone so terribly wrong that he'd left the forces and settled on a dairy farm in the middle of nowhere?

And then there was the sticking point—he'd used Crystal and openly admitted it.

"My sister paid the price," she replied quietly.

"Your sister had her own reasons for what happened that weekend," he answered calmly. "Or did you not know that?"

It burned that he presumed to know more about Crystal than she had. For years they'd only had each other, shared an apartment, shared secrets. He'd known Crystal all of three days.

"Don't tell me about her," she answered, her voice shaking a little. "I think I know my own sister. Knew," she amended immediately. It was so difficult to remember to talk about Crystal in the past tense.

"Then you knew she had a thing for Pete and that being asked to be Elizabeth's maid of honor was a slap in the face."

"Don't be ridiculous. They were best friends."

But deep down Avery got the squirmy sensation that he might be right. Now that she thought about it, Crystal had always acted different when Pete and Elizabeth were around. Quieter, more subdued.

"Avery?"

His voice brought her back to the present. "Sorry," she said automatically.

"It's fine. I just…we were both messed up, that's all. But we knew it. Neither of us pretended it was something it wasn't."

She didn't want to hear the details. "Did you regret it? Afterward, I mean." For some reason that was the one thing she wanted to know. Crystal had always maintained that it was mutual, but during the first days of the pregnancy she'd been so upset at the idea of being a mother. Angry at having her life change…

He looked down at his plate. "That's an impossible question for me to answer. It…is what it is. But I am sorry she's gone, truly. She was a nice girl. How did it happen?"

Maybe it was coming a little late, but at least he was asking. Thinking about it still caused Avery's heart to hurt. "She had a rare heart condition that showed up after she delivered Nell. They call it *peripartum cardiomyopathy*. She was so tired, and her ankles swelled during her last few weeks of pregnancy. She was having a hard time breathing, but we all just chalked it up to being so close to delivery, you know? But it wasn't. They said it was very treatable, but then…she was just gone. She was one of the small percentage that just…" She gulped around the lump in her throat. "The official term is 'sudden cardiac death.'" She reached for her water glass, surprised to find her fingers trembling. It was still too fresh—the pain and shock of losing her beautiful and vibrant sister.

Callum reached over and took her hand. "It doesn't always make sense," he said, squeezing her fingers. "One moment people you care about are there, and the next… they just aren't anymore. Trying to figure it out will only make you crazy. You just have to find a way to go on."

The tightness in his voice told her he might just have some experience in that department, but she didn't want to know. Didn't want to get too close to Callum. It would only muddy the waters.

"I have to go on," she said, blinking back the tears that had formed in her eyes. "For Nell. I'm all she's got." *She's all I've got, too*, Avery thought, but she kept silent about that.

She looked down and realized that she'd twined her fingers with Callum's, her pale, slender fingers dwarfed by his rough, workingman hands. Embarrassed and with a strange lightness in her stomach, she pulled her hand away.

He didn't contradict her. Despite the cautious sharing that had happened over the meal, despite the assurance that he claimed Nell as his daughter, she knew that if he were truly committed, he would have said something like *she's got me, too.*

But he didn't. He didn't say *anything.*

It made Avery feel more alone than she had in a very long time.

"There's pie for dessert," he offered, but the invitation sounded forced and a lot like a consolation prize.

"None for me, thanks," she said, eager now to escape. "I'm still on Ontario time. It's after eleven back home. I'll help you clean up and then I think I'll go to bed. Nell will be up early."

He pushed his chair away from the table. "You don't need to clean up, you're company. Go. I'll look after this."

"You're sure?" she asked.

"Go," he repeated, and she felt her cheeks flame. He couldn't be clearer about wanting to keep his distance, could he?

It was going to be a long two weeks.

CHAPTER FIVE

By 8:00 A.M. Avery was ready to go back to bed. Her eyes burned and her lashes felt gritty each time she blinked. She didn't know if it was the strange place or what, but Nell had been up every three hours during the night. Now Avery had been up since six, and the coffeepot was down to half.

She hadn't seen Callum at all. When Nell began crying at six, she'd heard him go out the front door. No doubt he was regretting asking them to stay.

Now Nell was sound asleep, her little face peaceful as she lay in Avery's arms. "Little monkey," Avery murmured, half exasperated and half with affection. The baby had to be exhausted. If Avery hadn't slept, neither had Nell. And neither, probably, had Callum.

Sitting in the big armchair in his living room, Avery let her eyes drift closed. If she could just sneak a few minutes…

The sound of boots being stomped and the slam of the door jolted her awake. When she jumped, so did Nell, and then her tiny face crumpled up and a pitiful wail echoed through the room.

Avery sighed.

"Sorry," Callum offered. "I didn't know you'd be sleeping."

She bit back the sharp retort sitting on her lips and

looked over her shoulder at him. Truthfully he hadn't made that much noise, it was just that it sounded so abrupt in the early morning silence. There was nothing to compete with it—no traffic, no planes overhead, no people on the sidewalk or even a softly playing radio.

Avery couldn't remember the last time she'd heard this much silence. She looked up and realized he looked as tired as she felt.

"Did you sleep at all?" she asked.

"Not much," he admitted.

"She's not usually this fussy. I don't know what came over her last night. I mean, she's not sleeping through the night and she's been waking a little more often lately, but last night was..."

She sighed again. "Sorry" was all she could think to say.

"It's okay. I had to get up and do the milking anyway."

The barn was probably ten times more peaceful than the house.

Nell settled down and her lids started drooping again. "Let me try to put her on the bed," Avery said. "I'll be right back."

The baby settled into the soft covers instantly and Avery placed a pillow on either side of her just in case Nell managed what she hadn't yet—rolling. When she went back to the kitchen Callum was pouring a fresh cup of coffee into his travel mug.

"Have you had breakfast?" she asked.

"Not yet. What would you like?"

"Oh, I'll cook it. Good heavens, I don't intend for you to wait on me. If you don't mind, that is."

"If you cook better than me it's not a problem at all," he added, stirring milk into his coffee.

She passed by him and opened the fridge, surprised by this new equanimity, wondering if they were both so tired it simply took too much energy to be awkward. "Eggs, then? How do you like them?"

"I'm not fussy," he answered.

"Great." She took out eggs, butter and a package of sliced ham she found in the deli drawer. There were mushrooms and peppers in the crisper and she took those out, too, and a hunk of cheddar. "Omelets work for you?"

"Perfect."

She found a bowl and began cracking and whisking eggs together with a fork. While she put the vegetables to sauté, Callum got out plates and put bread in the toaster.

"You like cooking, huh," he commented.

She put the veggies in a bowl and poured half the egg batter into the hot pan. "Yeah, I do."

"So why cakes?"

She grinned. "Come on, cake? Everyone loves cake. I mean, I like cooking, period, but I really love working with the icing and coming up with pretty decorations and stuff."

"Like that show, *Cake Boss?*"

She laughed again, amazed that Mr. Reclusive even had cable let alone had heard of the popular show. "No, nothing as fancy as that. They do some crazy stuff on there. And wedding cakes definitely aren't my specialty, at least not yet. I leave that to my boss, Denise. Right now I'm practicing on using more molding chocolate and fondant to add touches. And experimenting with flavors. I'm really good at the cupcakes. A unique flavor, a swirl of buttercream..."

She broke off, realizing Callum was just standing there looking at her. "I get carried away." She felt a blush heat her cheeks as she turned back to the stove.

"You're doing something you love. Nothing wrong with that. Too many people find themselves in careers they hate. Maybe we have something in common after all."

"You?"

She turned around in surprise, but he just shrugged. "The military wasn't for me. I wasn't as good at taking orders as I should have been. I kind of like to do my own thing. Farming suits me down to the ground."

He sounded as if he meant it.

"But it's so…" She looked down at his jeans.

"Dirty?" he supplied dryly.

A smile crept up her cheek. "Well, yeah."

"Nothing wrong with honest dirt," he answered. "First thing in the morning, when I go out to do the milking, I get to watch the sun rise over the prairie." Suddenly he grinned. "You could have done that this morning, too, you were up early enough."

The sight of Callum smiling made her catch her breath. This was a glimpse of the man she'd met ever so briefly the year before. It wasn't just the smile, either. Little crinkles appeared at the tanned corners of his eyes and they seemed to light up, sparkling at her from the other side of the kitchen. They were deep-set and nearly black when he frowned, but the morning light picked up bits of warm chocolate and caramel.

She spent far too long analyzing the varied depths and realized with some embarrassment that she'd been staring. The omelet was ready to be flipped so she grabbed the spatula and turned it over, thankful that her back was to him now. "You can put the toast down," she said softly. "This is almost done."

When his was ready she slid it onto a waiting plate and began the same process for the next. By the time it was done Callum had a plate with eight slices of buttered toast on it and had poured her a glass of apple juice.

"Who on earth are you feeding?" she asked, staring at all the bread.

He just reached for the jam. "I'm a good eater." He

angled her a glance and then put his attention back to his plate. "You could stand to eat a bit, too."

He thought she was too thin? She was conscious about her figure, of course she was. And she did test all her new recipes to make sure they were up to snuff. But never had anyone accused her of being too thin.

"I eat," she answered. "And speaking of, if Nell and I are going to be here for the next while, it's only fair that I help out. I don't want to take advantage of your hospitality. I thought I'd take a run into town later and pick up a few things, if you don't mind me borrowing your truck. I'll look after the meals while I'm here, how does that sound?"

He shrugged. "It sounds better than my cooking, that's for sure."

Satisfied, she sat back. The last thing she wanted to be was a freeloader. He'd already thought that she was after child support. She didn't mean to be a leech as well.

Besides, she felt she had something to prove.

When the meal was over she went to work clearing away the dishes while Callum disappeared into a third bedroom that he'd converted into a mini-office. By the time the frying pan was washed, Nell was up again.

Avery closed her eyes and sighed. She wasn't going to catch a break all day, was she?

By ten o'clock she was ready to pull out her hair. Nell wasn't content to do anything, so Avery finally decided to take her outside for a walk around the property. The previous owner had planted some rosebushes that were still blooming, their scent sweet in the air. They examined those, then discovered a bird's nest in some scrub brush, and then, to Avery's surprise, came upon Callum's vegetable garden.

It wasn't large, but the plants looked green and healthy. She could make out the tall tomato plants, cucumber vines, tangled peas and pert beans. Some of the beans were long and fat and ready to be picked, and the peas were just starting to fill out their pods.

Callum was squatted down in the middle of it all, pulling weeds away from the beans.

"Nice garden," she called to him.

He put his hands on his knees and pushed himself up, tipping back his ball cap. "It's coming. Beans are just about ripe, peas'll be along anytime."

"You really do like the outdoors, don't you?" She shifted Nell on her arm.

"I couldn't do this if I didn't. Come on in and have a look."

"But the fence..." Callum had protected the garden from any animals who might enjoy nibbling on his harvest by constructing a fence of wood stakes and chicken wire.

He held out a hand. "It's not too high. Step over sideways." He brushed his hands on his jeans. "Here, I'll take Nell."

She handed over the baby, her heart taking a surprise bump as she saw him holding his daughter for the first time. Once Nell was in the crook of his arm, he held out his hand again, presumably to help her over.

She took it and her heart bumped again at the feeling of his fingers tightening over hers. She swung one leg over the wire and then her second, giving a little hop at the end. Callum's dry chuckle teased her ears and she found herself smiling.

"Your legs are longer than mine," she chided. She was going to put out her hands to take Nell back but decided not to. Nell was happy and Callum looked comfortable.

"The grand tour," he said, pointing. "Potatoes, then onions there. Then peas, beans, carrots, lettuce and spinach, and cucumbers and tomatoes at the far end."

He squatted down and plucked a weed, tossing it into a bucket. "One of the things I missed when I was in the forces was having a garden. We always had one at home."

"And home was where?" she asked, realizing she really didn't know a lot about him.

"Lower mainland of B.C., not far from Abbotsford. That's where my uncle had his farm."

"And you have a sister, you said?"

He nodded as they walked slowly past the rows of green vegetables. "My baby sister, Taylor, who's twenty-five. And a brother, Jack, who's twenty-eight."

"Are you close?"

Callum avoided looking at her and bent to pull out another weed, Nell still securely on his arm. "Not as close as we used to be. I was gone a lot with the forces, and ended up settling here while they still live close to Vancouver."

Avery felt sad for him. Whatever had caused the change, he'd also isolated himself from his family because of it. She frowned. "You still have a chance to connect again," she said.

Callum looked at her then, as if he understood what she didn't say: that she wouldn't ever have that chance with Crystal.

"You're right, of course," he replied. "And I suppose at some point I'm going to have to tell them they're an aunt and uncle."

Nell picked that moment to fuss, so Avery held out her arms. "I should get her in out of the sun. Her skin's so tender and I don't want her to burn. Maybe I can take a cucumber and tomato with me and put them in the fridge for our lunch?"

"Good idea." He plucked one of each off the vines and once she was safely over the fence, handed them to her.

It had felt remarkably normal, talking with him in the

sun. She'd liked talking to him, touching his hand, seeing Nell on his arm.

Liked it perhaps a little too much.

Avery was just thinking about taking that run into town when a puff of dust rose up from the dirt lane. She looked out the window to see two huge trucks pulling up, each towing a wagon of hay. They pulled up beside the barn and Avery was fascinated as the drivers hopped out—tall, rangy men in jeans, like Callum, and both wearing broad-brimmed Stetsons.

She really was in cowboy country, wasn't she?

A bigger surprise was when the passenger-side door on one of the trucks opened up and a woman got out. Avery's heart began to race. Nell pulled a chunk of her hair but she couldn't even bother to disentangle the tiny fingers from the strands. Instead she watched Callum come out of the barn and shake hands with the men. He spoke to the woman, too, and they all turned and looked her way.

Avery stepped back from the window.

When she peeked through the curtains again she could see the woman coming toward the house.

Okay. This was not a disaster. After all, Avery wasn't the one who was supposed to be all paranoid about the grapevine; that was Callum. She was a guest, that was all. She scrambled to come up with possible answers to the predictable questions when there was a tap on the door.

She had to answer it. It would look stupid if she didn't.

Nell was still on her hip when she opened the door and pasted on a smile. "Hi," she said, giving Nell a bounce to adjust her weight better.

"Hi, you're Avery, right? I'm Clara, Tyson Diamond's wife."

Clara Diamond was pretty in an unassuming sort of

way—beautiful blond curls that ended at her shoulders, an easy smile and big blue eyes that exuded friendliness. Avery stepped aside. "Come on in."

"I hope you don't mind. Ty and Sam said they were coming out here this morning to bring Callum a load of hay and I asked if I could come along for the ride. Molly—that's their mom—offered to watch our daughter for an hour or two. It's quite something to be able to step away for an hour or two. Just a drive with Ty is something special, you know? A chance to talk without interruption." She grinned. "I'll take whatever couple-time I can get, especially this time of year."

Avery nodded, not knowing what else to do. It was clear as could be that Clara was besotted with her husband. "I'm sure alone time is a precious commodity," she answered, thinking she sounded silly. How would she know? Avery had never even really been in love before. She believed in it but wasn't sure she'd ever find it for herself. Especially now. Being a single mom put a big kink in a girl's social life.

"Anyway, Callum mentioned he had guests and that you might like some company while they unload the hay. And who have we here?" She reached out and touched Nell's cheek with a finger. "Oh, my, aren't you precious. What's your name, sweetheart?"

Avery found herself warming to the woman. After all, she was refreshingly friendly and anyone who made a fuss of Nell was automatically moved up a few steps in her book. "This is Janell."

"She's adorable." Clara looked back at Avery. "Pardon me for being nosy, but are you and Callum…"

Avery shook her head quickly. "Oh, no. Callum is… an old friend of my sister's. Nell and I are heading back to Ontario soon."

"Your sister?" Clara's brows puckered. "Wow. Okay. It's just that, well, for a minute there I was going to say that Nell was the picture of Callum, with those big eyes and dark curls."

Avery had to turn away for a moment as her emotions surged. Someone else besides her and Callum could see the resemblance.

"Do you want a cup of coffee or anything?" she asked, walking toward the kitchen. "I'm afraid I don't have much else to offer at the moment. Nell and I were just going to take a trip to town."

"Just water's fine," Clara answered.

When she returned, Clara was still standing in the small foyer. "Oh, for heaven's sake," Avery said, embarrassed. "I'm sorry, Mrs. Diamond. Come on in and sit down. I'm afraid I didn't get much sleep last night and I'm not firing on all cylinders this morning."

Clara took the glass of water and sat in a chair. "First time teething?"

Avery looked up with a start. "Teething?"

"You didn't know?" Clara grinned. "Not sleeping so great at night? Drooling a lot and chewing?"

"Well, yes, but…how did you know?"

"The rosy cheeks were a dead giveaway. Honestly when Susanna was around four and a half months we had the first two teeth come all at once. Not fun."

"Nell's my first…I really didn't know. Will it last long?"

Clara laughed. "Until it breaks through. If you go to the drugstore in town, the pharmacist can give you some baby acetaminophen for the fever and some gel for her gums. I discovered a teething ring that was great—and bought three. I'd put them in the freezer. When the first one got warm, I'd take out another. The cool soothes the gums."

Avery was awash with gratitude. "Thanks for the advice. I appreciate it. I definitely don't want to keep Callum up again tonight."

"Or yourself, either," Clara said with a smile. "So what brings you to Cadence Creek?"

Avery paused, scrambling to come up with something that sounded plausible. Clara's eyes softened. "If I'm being rude for someone you just met, tell me. But she's his, isn't she?"

Avery knew she should tell Clara to mind her own business, but there was no judgment in her tone, nothing but kindness. "Yeah," she said softly, watching as Nell rammed her fist in her mouth and gnawed on it. Teething indeed. How had she missed that?

"And yours?"

Avery's gaze snapped up. "Oh! No, she's not. She really is my sister's baby. But my sister died after giving birth, so now..." Her throat clogged up. "Now I get to be her mama."

Clara's huge eyes softened. "Oh, I'm so sorry. How horrible for you. And Callum didn't know?"

Avery shook her head. "He's just getting used to the idea," she admitted.

Clara put her glass down on the coffee table. "She's the spitting image of him! Well, except for the perma-scowl."

Avery laughed despite herself. She could really like this Clara—but it wasn't like they'd ever have time to become friends.

"Give him time," Clara said. "Gotta be a shock to open the door and find out you're a father. When I got pregnant it freaked Ty out big-time."

"Well, I don't want anything from Callum. I just wanted him to know. I didn't feel right keeping it all a secret." She kissed Nell's downy head.

"Well," Clara said, "as much as I'd love to stay and chat, I should probably see how the boys are getting along. I wanted to ask Ty to run me into town for a few minutes before we head home."

"I'm going that way," Avery offered. "I can take you in if you want, and Ty can pick you up when he's done."

Clara smiled. "That'd be great! I'll let him know while you grab your stuff."

They chatted about Cadence Creek on the drive into town, and Avery dropped Clara off at the bank while she went on to the pharmacy and grocery store. She'd only been in town a few days, but already she remembered where most of the shops were, and she took a moment to linger at the general store, where she bought a dish of ice cream. She even gave Nell a taste off the tip of her plastic spoon, laughing as the baby smacked her lips.

But the whole time she could hear Clara's voice saying how Nell was the very image of Callum, and she couldn't erase the image of Callum holding Nell in his arms from her mind.

Avery figured there wasn't any point in sitting idly by while Callum worked. She needed to keep busy, so she brushed the fresh chicken she'd bought with some oil and seasoning and put it to bake, then washed some potatoes for baking, peeled carrots and chopped some fresh dill to sprinkle on them. There was nothing more to do for supper until much closer to the time, and she was left twiddling her thumbs again.

And still Nell slept, finally soothed by the medicine the pharmacist had given her.

Avery was going to go crazy if this was the way her days were going to go for the next few weeks. There was nothing that made her feel better than baking, so she got out the basic ingredients she'd bought to make a fancy bread. She hummed as she worked, mashing up a few over-ripe bananas, mixing them with oil and sugar, flour and eggs. The recipe was one she knew by heart and in no time flat a banana bread was in the oven beside the chicken.

By the time the mess was tidied, Nell was up. After a quick diaper change Avery put her on the play mat. The bread came out of the oven, the chicken was basted, the potatoes went in and after she'd set the table, she put the carrots on.

If she were home right now, she wouldn't be making a simple chicken dinner. She'd be decorating cupcakes for two hundred or constructing delicate sugar flowers. She'd be listening to the other bakers chatter and hear the muf- fled noise of the storefront through the swinging doors.

The Icing on Top was the best job she'd ever had. This was all well and good for a week or two, but she missed the regular commotion of her life. The vitality. The purpose.

Callum came in from milking. Dinner was a quiet af- fair, and afterward Avery took Nell for a bath. Holding her steady in the tub while trying to wash all the nooks and crannies was a challenge, and Avery missed the con- venience of the baby tub at home. But Nell didn't seem to mind one bit. She babbled and splashed happily in the water, getting Avery soaked and having a marvelous time.

There was water all over the floor by the time they were done. Avery ran a towel over it after she'd dressed Nell in a pair of pink cotton sleepers. She was just running a tiny comb through the soft, dark hair when Callum appeared in the doorway.

He leaned against the frame, watching them in the mirror for a moment, making Avery's pulse quicken even though she knew he must be watching Nell and not her.

"There," Avery said brightly. "Spic and span for at least ten minutes!"

Callum smiled. Avery was starting to recognize that

he wasn't ever the big, wide smile kind of guy, but that a small upturn of his lips meant the same thing. Right now the corners of his mouth were turned up and his eyes were lit with good humor.

"You got just as wet as she did, I think."

Avery looked down. Her blouse was covered in damp splotches and her trousers clung to her legs in wet spots. "I think you're right."

"So what happens now? This is all bedtime routine, right?"

"Bath, then some playtime until she's getting tired, and then a bottle before bed. The time change has screwed things up a bit, but I try to get her down around ten or so. That way she only gets up once in the night." Avery smiled back at him, happy he was taking an interest. "It used to be down at nine, up at midnight, up at three, up at six. If I can get it to ten-two-six then I still get a good night's sleep. Maybe one of these days she'll shock me and sleep through the night."

Avery scooted by him and went out to the living room. The play mat was still on the floor and she placed Nell on it. "At home," she explained, "I have this activity center that she can look up at while she's on her mat. It'll be better once she's sitting up on her own. Usually I end up handing her toys over and over while reading or watching something on TV."

True to her word, Nell's chubby fingers grabbed on to a rattle and she shook it, her eyes widening with excitement at the sound.

"I can watch her for a bit. Why don't you go have your own bath? You must not get many minutes to yourself."

Avery didn't know what to say. It was incredibly thoughtful. "I don't," she admitted. "I mean, I can after she goes to bed, but…"

"But you're always listening for her."

She was surprised he realized that. "Yeah. Besides, what about the kitchen? There are dishes…"

"I did them while you were bathing Nell. Least I could do after you cooked."

She blinked. He'd worked outside all day and he still came in and did dishes? Callum was turning out to be full of surprises. Or maybe there was just a nicer guy underneath the giant chip he carried on his shoulder.

"Go," he said. "Enjoy it."

"What if…" She didn't know how to finish the question. He had offered to give her precious time alone. But he'd never been alone with a baby before. With Nell. She frowned.

"If there's something I can't handle, I'll knock on the door," he said. "Seriously. Run a bath."

She did. Callum's bathroom wasn't stocked with flowery toiletries, so she added a dollop of her shampoo to the water in lieu of bubble bath and filled it up with steaming hot water. She even grabbed a magazine she'd bought at the airport and hadn't read.

The water felt wonderful and she let out a long sigh. And before she even got past the table of contents, her eyelids began to droop.

CHAPTER SIX

CALLUM SPENT SEVERAL minutes sitting on the floor, handing Nell her rattle and a stuffed dog and a set of plastic keys over and over. It was amazing how her eyes focused on his face so intently, as if she were trying to read his mind. "Hi," he said softly, feeling stupid. How did someone talk to a baby? Her little arms and legs flailed about, but she seemed happy. Her cheeks were the same soft pink as her pajamas. And she looked so tiny.

"Hi, Nell," he tried again. "I'm your daddy."

The words sounded impossible to his ears, but then she gave a big kick and her tiny lips curved up in what could only be classified as a smile.

Something stirred inside him.

No sounds came from the bathroom where Avery was soaking in a bath. As Nell played, Callum's thoughts drifted to think of his daughter's aunt. He'd meant what he said today. He fully recognized that she'd turned her life upside down for her niece. For him. She could have gone on with her life and not let on any differently, but instead she'd come to him with the truth even though it had to have been a difficult thing to do.

He respected her for that. Even if he hadn't liked her at first, he'd respected that honesty. Especially when he'd finally admitted to himself that she *was* being honest and not trying to put something over on him.

Nell started to fuss and Callum turned his head, looking at the bathroom door. He didn't want to disturb Avery—especially in the tub. He swallowed. She was on the other side of that door right now, naked, her slender limbs slick with hot water and bubbles. It made him wonder. Made images pop into his head that had no right to be there. She had mentioned a job but no one special in her life. Was there? Had there ever been? As far as he could tell, there hadn't been any mysterious calls to her cell during the days she'd been here.

The discontented squawks turned to cries and Callum knew he was going to have to do it sometime—he was going to have to try feeding her. Carefully he put one hand beneath Nell's bottom and the other beneath her head as he'd seen Avery do. He lifted her up and placed her against his shoulder, his nostrils filled with the sweet baby-lotion scent of her.

She was impossibly light.

And she immediately grabbed a chunk of his hair and pulled hard enough to make his eyes water. Now he understood why Avery put her hair up so often. He disentangled her fingers and went to the kitchen in search of a bottle. He'd watched Avery earlier so figured he had to heat it a bit. He ran some hot water and stuck the bottle in a container while wandering around the kitchen. When it was finally warm, he went back into the living room and settled into the recliner, adjusting Nell's weight on his arm.

Nell took the nipple in her mouth, her wide, blue eyes looking up at him with absolute trust as she placed one hand possessively on the bottle.

His heart turned over. He was feeding his child. All the hopes that he'd tamped down, the feelings he'd battled through when he'd found out Jane was pregnant came rushing back. Back then it had felt like everything was possible. A woman he loved. Starting a family. Everything just the way he'd planned.

But it had all been a mistake, a charade. And if he appreciated one thing about Avery it was that she was, at least, honest to a fault.

Unlike Jane, who'd been nothing but a liar.

Wrong, a voice inside his head contradicted. *She did tell the truth eventually.*

But not soon enough. The truth had taken his life and blown it to smithereens. And now Jane was living in some fancy house in Vancouver with her fancy architect husband and they probably had fancy two-point-five kids and a fancy dog.

Tiny hands were waving again and he realized he'd pulled the bottle away from her lips. He made a silly face and shook his head and she laughed, a bubble of a giggle that seemed to come right from the middle of her belly. He grinned and did it again. And then squinted as he stared at her gums. Could it be?

He ran his index finger over her bottom gum and felt the sharp edge of a tooth. No wonder she'd been happier today. A tiny tooth had broken through! Her first one.

She started to suck on his finger so he quickly gave her the bottle back. Just then he heard the sound of the tub draining and tried to block out the mental image of Avery getting out of the bath and drying herself with a thick cotton towel.

A few minutes later Avery came out, her skin flushed and glowing from the heat and moisture of the bathroom. She wore a simple T-shirt and a pair of light cotton pajama bottoms. Her feet were bare and there was a sheepish look on her face.

"How is she? I fell asleep in the tub."

"Almost done her bottle."

Avery's mouth dropped open as she stepped forward. "You fed her?"

He nodded. "Yep. Heated the bottle a little first, I hope it was enough. She didn't seem to mind."

Avery's gaze seemed glued to the sight of Nell in his arms. "She's really fine, Avery."

"I can see that." Her voice sounded tight.

"Oh, and guess what?" He looked up at her. "She's got her first tooth! That must be why she didn't cry as much today, right? And you said she slept great this afternoon."

Avery came forward and he took the bottle out of Nell's mouth. She felt along the gum line with a finger and smiled. "You're right! Well, how about that."

There was something else in her voice, a wistfulness he didn't quite understand. "Do you want me to put her to bed?"

Not just wistfulness. For some reason his simple question looked as if it pained her.

"You should probably burp her first, so she doesn't have gas."

"Oh. Right."

He handed Avery the nearly empty bottle and lifted Nell to his shoulder. He began patting her lightly, alarmed at the size of his hand on her tiny back, but Avery chuckled. "Don't be afraid to give it a good pat," she said. "You won't hurt her."

He patted a little harder, encouraged by Avery's nod.

Nell gave a tiny burp and he smiled, pleased at his parental prowess. She smiled back at him—and then to his surprise there was a different sort of gurgling sound and he found his shoulder covered in spit-up.

* * *

Avery's mouth dropped open at his surprised expression as a much-relieved Nell relaxed in his arms—arms that had tensed now that his shoulder was covered in formula.

Talk about baptism by fire into fatherhood!

"Oh, my word," she breathed with utter dismay, stepping forward to collect Nell. "Oh, Callum."

She took the baby who, other than a small dribble of sour milk, remained unscathed.

His lips twitched. And before she had time to prepare for it, he was laughing. A full-out laugh that rumbled up and out of his chest.

He had a shirt coated in baby vomit and he was laughing. The sight of it hit her square in the gut. He was a different man when he let go of whatever it was that bogged him down. When he smiled…when he laughed, a rich, full chuckle with a hint of a gravelly rasp, everything seemed to warm in the room. She couldn't help it, she started to laugh, too. And the more she laughed, the harder he did until they were both wiping their eyes.

"I'm so sorry," she gasped.

He grinned, pinching the fabric in two fingers and holding it away from himself. "Oh, don't be. I'm a farmer, remember? I've been covered in much worse."

"Give her time. You haven't tried diapers yet…"

And they both burst out laughing again.

Nell was rubbing her eyes now, burrowing into Avery's shoulder. "She feels better, if it's any consolation."

"It is," he answered. "Why don't you put her down while I go change?"

"Okay."

He disappeared into his room while Avery rocked back and forth, swinging her hips lightly from side to side. It was getting late; she'd stayed in the tub far too long and it was dark outside. Definitely time that Nell was in bed, and it seemed to only take a moment or two and her lashes were drifting lazily toward her cheeks. Avery went into the bedroom and laid her carefully in the playpen and covered her up with a blanket. She should probably go to bed, too, but the nap in the tub had revitalized her. Instead she made her way back down the hall.

The bathroom door was ajar when she went by and she was going to turn the light off when she saw Callum through the opening. He was unbuttoning his shirt, slipping the buttons from the holes one by one until it gaped open at the waist.

She swallowed.

Then he shrugged it off, first the sticky shoulder and then the other, revealing a lean, strong chest. His jeans sat low on his hips and she could just make out the tiniest glimpse of the band of his underwear.

He was her niece's father, but it didn't matter to her body, which responded on a completely physical level to the sight of him standing shirtless in the bathroom.

She scooted away before she could make a fool of herself, and went outside on the porch where the air was blessedly cool.

She should have gone home. It would have been easier than agreeing to spend two weeks sharing a house with Callum Shepard. It was even worse now, because there wasn't the same anger between them. Not only had he called Nell by her name, but he'd played with her, held her, fed her. He'd been thrown up on and instead of being angry or grossed out he'd laughed.

He'd offered her a break. And if that wasn't enough, she'd seen him stripped to the waist in all his muscled glory.

How was she supposed to remain immune to that?

The evening was calm, with a quiet breeze that whispered through the leaves of the trees. Avery sat on the porch step, her arms around her knees as she breathed in the summer air. Across the lawn fireflies flickered, and she watched them for a few minutes, trying to figure out how she felt about what had just happened. Not just Callum and this attraction she couldn't seem to shake. But his new, active role with Nell. She would never admit it to him but she'd felt jealousy seeing her baby girl in his arms. Annoyance that she'd spent months with Nell and he'd spent barely an hour, but he'd been the one to discover her first tooth. Avery felt those firsts were hers by right.

She was feeling rather selfish when all was said and done. But at least she realized it. In a few weeks when they went home, she'd have Nell all to herself. It would be terrible to deny Callum those moments now, when their time was so short. Who knew when he'd see her again?

She'd just made peace with her feelings when the screen door opened and shut again quietly. "Nice night," he said softly, coming to sit beside her on the step.

There was a slight clinking sound and he handed her a bottle. "Beer?"

She took the bottle from his hand, surprised. Together they took a drink and she sighed, leaning her shoulder against the post that anchored the stair railing. "Thanks," she said. "I don't remember the last time I kicked back with a beer."

"I owe you an apology," he said softly. Avery could only make out the outline of his features in the dark, but she didn't doubt the sincerity in his words.

"For what?" she asked.

"For being so hard on you when you first arrived. I don't trust very easily, you see."

"But you trust me now?"

"I want to, and that's a fairly new feeling."

"It'd be pretty low to lie about the paternity of an innocent child," she responded.

He turned his head to stare at her, and even in the dark she could see the sparks in his eyes. After a moment or two they tempered, but she understood very quickly that her words had touched a nerve somehow. But she wasn't going to ask. She wasn't sure she wanted to know. If it was bad then she might come to regret her decision to make him part of Nell's life. And if it was something painful...

Well. She really didn't want to start *liking* him. Add that to the physical awareness thing and it could get messy. And that was no way to run a custody arrangement. She had to keep things as clear and as uncomplicated as possible.

He turned away and took another drink from his bottle, then rested his elbows on his knees.

"I was engaged once," he said abruptly.

Avery swallowed, knowing it was an invitation but reluctant to accept it. "I see," she answered carefully.

"No, of course you don't see," he contradicted. "How can you?"

"You want to talk about it?" The question seemed ludicrous. Callum? Chatting about feelings? Talk about your major surprises.

"Not really. But maybe I want you to understand what happened with Crystal last year. And why I acted like I did when you knocked on my door."

Crystal. When it came right down to it, it was hard to forget that this man and her sister had hooked up after knowing each other for, what, twenty-four hours?

Callum sighed. "Six months before Pete and Elizabeth's wedding, I was engaged to a woman named Jane. I was back from a deployment and the first thing I did was go out and buy her a ring. We were planning our wedding in a rush because I wanted to be married before I had to leave to go overseas again. The church was booked, Jane had her dress, we'd chosen the menu for the reception... and Jane dropped the bombshell that she was pregnant."

Avery swallowed. She knew he was trying to be all matter-of-fact about it but she could hear the underlying pain in his voice.

"I was happy about the baby. It was unexpected, sure, but we were getting married anyway. Our wedding date was only three months away, so I didn't see the problem with her showing already. But Jane insisted that we move up the date, so we trimmed the guest list, booked a Justice of the Peace instead of the church and we planned a lower-key event for six weeks later."

His voice changed, hardened. "One week before the wedding Jane came to me and said she couldn't go through with it."

Avery had known this was coming. Clearly there was no wife or baby here so it hadn't worked out. Which begged the question, where were they now? How could he have abandoned his child like that?

"She broke your heart," Avery said quietly.

"She broke everything about me," he admitted. "You see, the reason why she didn't want to wait was because her pregnancy was further along than she'd said."

"I don't understand." Avery's brows pulled together. If they'd moved up the date because of the pregnancy, why call it off?

And then she understood, and all the pieces started clicking together. Oh, poor Callum. "How much further along?" she asked cautiously.

Even in the darkness she saw a muscle tick in his jaw. "I was still in Afghanistan. And it wasn't a miracle conception."

"The baby wasn't yours." A heavy feeling settled on her chest. "But she'd been going to let you think it was." "Exactly." Callum drained what was left in his bottle and then turned it over and over absently in his hands. "She'd had an affair while I was on deployment, but when I got back she felt too guilty to break it off with me. *What kind of girl does that,* she said. *Breaks up with her man the moment he's back home?* And then I proposed…it was all very difficult for her, you see. She didn't know how to let me down easy." Bitterness bled through his voice. "She had an attack of conscience at the eleventh hour, told me the truth and a week later kept the appointment with the Justice of the Peace, just with a different groom."

Avery bit down on her lip. This Jane had gone ahead with their lives together only with someone else in Callum's spot. "This was how long before Pete's wedding?"

"Not long enough. I tried to put on a good show for Pete but I was not in a wedding frame of mind. To me it was all a sham. And then I met your sister and she was pretending, too, because she'd been secretly in love with Pete for years. I'm not saying what we did was right, but I'm saying we were both looking for a distraction to get through it and we found it in each other. I never meant to leave her with a baby, Avery. I wouldn't have been that careless, especially after what I went through with Jane."

"And so when I showed up at the door…"

"All I could think about was Jane, asking me to move up the wedding because she was pregnant and it wasn't even my kid. I'd known Jane for years. If she could lie to me that easily, why couldn't a complete stranger?"

"That's why you wanted the paternity proof."

"Yeah."

Avery put down her beer bottle, the taste of it suddenly bitter. "What changed it for you?"

He shrugged. "I was trying to ignore what was right before my eyes—right up until when you started to drive away. I knew deep down that she was mine." His eyes looked into hers. "What kind of man would I be if I let her go like that?"

Avery tried not to sigh out loud, but her heart felt it just the same. It was hard to resist a man who admitted he was flawed and then turned around and did what was right.

"I'm glad you came after us," she said, knowing it was true even if it did cause complications. "We'll figure all this out. I want her to know you, Callum. To know she has a dad who cares."

"You're a good mother, Avery. I'm sorry I said what I did the first day. There's more to mothering than whether or not you birthed her. I know that."

He really had to stop now before she turned into a complete puddle of goo. What she should really do was go inside. Go to bed and forget all about sitting outside with Callum Shepard in the moonlight. And yet she couldn't quite make herself get up and open that door. It was nice, she realized, just sitting and talking to someone. With the day-to-day care of Nell, it had been easier to pretend that she wasn't lonely. And before that she'd spent so much of her time with Crystal, planning for the baby, living through the pregnancy with her. Even being her delivery coach.

Avery looked over at him. "I saw Nell being born, you know. I was Crystal's birth coach. It was the scariest thing I've ever seen. And probably the most beautiful."

"I'm so sorry about her passing, you know. She was a good person. Beautiful and fun. You must miss her terribly."

Avery swallowed past a lump of emotion. "I do. She wasn't just my sister. She was my best friend."

Was she imagining things or had he somehow slid a little closer to her on the step?

"And what about other people? Is there anyone special?"

She laughed a little. "You mean like a boyfriend?"

"Is that a funny question?"

The beer was suddenly looking a little more attractive now and she picked the bottle up again and took a sip just to avoid answering.

"Avery?"

"Tell me something, Callum. When you were at the wedding, who did you notice? Me or Crystal?"

When he didn't answer, she nodded. "That's right. Of course it was Crystal. And why not? It's always been that way, and maybe that made it easier for me. I've never liked being the center of attention, you know. I was older than her, you see, and I spent a lot of time looking after her when we were growing up. Our mom worked a lot, so it fell to me to make sure Crystal was okay. If anything went wrong, I was the first one to get the blame. I should have known better, or should have been paying closer attention. So when we got older and the focus was suddenly on her, it was a relief, really. I was finally free to just do my own thing. The flip side of not being the center of attention is that you don't seem to get any."

"Ouch."

She shrugged. "Don't get me wrong, I dated some. Had a boyfriend a few years back but it turned out he was dating me just to get close to her. When I realized what was going on, I called it off, and when he made his move on her she kicked him to the curb quick enough. I never resented her for it. We had each other and we were family. Him, though—I was plenty mad at him for a long time. You don't play with people's feelings, you know?"

She gave him a sidelong glance. "Well, considering

what you told me, I guess you do know. Anyway, these days I'm too busy for a social life. And now I think that's probably enough sharing of our sordid pasts, don't you think?"

He chuckled, the sound low and intimate in the dark. "It's more than I've shared with anyone in a long time."

"I'm not sure whether to be honored or appalled."

He snorted. "I like that about you, Avery. You're not a pushover. You look all sweet and innocent but you've got a spine of steel."

He thought she was sweet? Innocent?

And strong. She thought she perhaps liked that best of all. Sometimes she wondered. She didn't feel strong. Most of the time she felt like she just had to keep pedaling to keep up.

"So why the sudden turnaround and baring of souls?"

He shrugged. "I guess I just figured that if we're going to make this work—me being a part of Nell's life and all—we need to make things civil. Friendly. Saying I was sorry and explaining my behavior seemed like a good start. I'm not usually so, well, rude."

He looked away from her, over the fields that spread out from the house. That same muscle ticked in his jaw again, and Avery got the sneaky feeling that there was more he wasn't telling her. But that was fine. They hardly knew each other. He had a right to his secrets.

"I think so, too," she answered softly. But the something else in the air, the something electric she couldn't quite define, made her wonder if it would ever be truly possible to be simply "civil" and "friendly" with him. He wasn't the kind of guy that screamed *platonic*. He was too...

Too tall, handsome, strong, enigmatic...

Oh, boy.

"I do remember you, you know," he admitted softly.

His voice had lowered even further, and it was as smooth as silk but with just a hint of texture that made it ride deliciously over her nerve endings.

"Remember me?" Why on earth did her voice come out all breathy-like? She took a deep breath and told herself to get a grip.

"From the wedding. On the boat you were off to one side, taking pictures instead of crowded around the railing. The poncho came down past your knees and the hood wouldn't stay up. And afterward when everyone was going to the casino, you wanted to stay back and walk through the Queen Victoria Garden."

She nearly swallowed her tongue. All this time she thought he didn't remember her. He'd pretended not to at first—to protect himself, she realized now. But he *had* noticed and she wasn't sure what to make of it.

"You remember all that?"

His dark gaze locked with hers. "I remember all of that. And thinking that I'd much rather spend a few hours walking with you in the fresh air among the trees and flowers than spend it in a loud, crazy casino."

His face seemed awfully close now, so close that her chest started to constrict and her stomach began turning nervous somersaults. Her gaze dropped to his lips… they were quite fine lips now that she examined them so closely. A puff of breeze ruffled his hair. "Why didn't you say so?" she breathed.

"Because I took one look at you and I knew," he replied, sitting back a bit, putting the tiniest bit of distance between them. "I knew that you weren't the kind of woman a man could flirt with and walk away from. Face it, Avery. You've got *lifer* written all over you. With you I would have been playing with feelings."

He stood up. "I don't play with feelings, Avery. And you were simply too complicated for a man like me."

With those parting words, he went inside and shut the door.

CHAPTER SEVEN

CALLUM TURNED THE last of the cows out into the pasture and spent the next half hour shoveling out the calf pen. He loved the baby calves, all big-eyed with soft noses and playful enough that they liked coming over for rubs on their heads. If things went well over the next few years, maybe he could apply to buy more quota, produce more milk. At least next year he'd be here for the whole growing season and he'd be able to put up a lot more of his own hay, rather than having to buy from local ranchers. He had plans.

This time next year, he realized, Nell would be walking. Probably saying her first words. And back in Ontario. He'd been there for this tooth but he'd miss all those other firsts. But what choice did he have? How could he possibly leave here just when he was getting started?

And then there was Avery to consider. Last night he'd come *this close* to kissing her, and that surprised him. Alarm was probably a better word for the feeling that had run through him this morning when he'd woke at dawn. He shouldn't be muddying the waters of the relationship. No, not relationship. Perhaps association was a better term for it. And he'd never intended to let on that he remembered her from that weekend in Niagara, or that he'd been tempted to spend the afternoon with her rather than with the rest of the wedding party at the casino.

But when she'd told him about the boyfriend who'd used her to get close to her sister, he'd felt badly for her. Crystal had been colorful, dynamic, outgoing. But Avery…

Hell, Avery was just as beautiful, just in a quieter, softer way. He'd meant what he said, too. She wasn't a fling kind of woman and he'd known that by looking at her. A fling was all he'd been prepared to offer, so when the rest of the group had decided to hit the slot machines and tables he'd gone along.

He shut the calf pen and made his way down through the barn. Right now he wasn't even prepared to offer a fling. Especially with Avery, because they had to keep things uncomplicated for Nell's sake.

So kissing her would have been a colossal mistake. Therefore it made no sense that he couldn't seem to shake the idea from his mind.

He stepped out into the sunshine and squinted, looking up at the house. He caught sight of her standing on his back step, hanging clothes on the line—her white trousers and blouse held up by pins and dancing lightly in the breeze, next to tiny white undershirts of Nell's, pink-footed sleepers and ruffled dresses barely bigger than his hand, and a line of his T-shirts and undershorts.

He watched as she lifted her arms to hang up another shirt, the angle throwing her breasts into relief and his mouth went dry. Very attractive in her own right when all was said and done.

All the self-talk in the world wasn't helping a damn bit. Because he still wanted to kiss her. Wanted to see if her lips were as soft as they appeared and if she'd blush the way he imagined.

He started walking toward the house, determined to

keep things on a level plane for the next several days. He could do that. It was just a momentary thing.

The aroma hit him the moment he stepped in the door. She'd been baking again and the entire place smelled like chocolate. He took off his boots by the door and went to the bathroom first to wash his hands, and then straight to the kitchen and the rich, cakey smell that teased his nostrils.

There were cupcakes covering an entire counter, like rows of mushroom-shaped soldiers, the stems wrapped in paper liners and the caps uniformly smooth and even. His mouth watered just looking at them, and he reached out and plucked one from the countertop, marring the perfect rows. He bit into it—it was still warm—and closed his eyes. It was perfection. And the second bite took him to a center that was smooth and rich like cheesecake.

"What in the world...caught with your hand in the cookie jar, I see!"

He spun around guiltily to find Avery standing with her hands on her hips, a smile flirting with her lips.

"Guilty as charged. These are fantastic."

"You could have waited for the frosting, you know."

"Don't need frosting. What in the world is in the middle?"

She grinned. "A cream cheese mixture."

"It's like cheesecake surrounded by cake." He popped the last bite in his mouth and would have reached for another except he caught the dangerous glint in her eye.

"Don't even think about it, buster. Wait for them to cool and I'll put the icing on."

"Chocolate icing?" He raised his eyebrows hopefully.

"Yes, chocolate icing. Very fudgy."

"What are you going to do with all of them? There must be three dozen here."

"Four," she corrected. "And I don't know. It's a lot for

two people. You could freeze them." She moved to the counter and started measuring icing sugar into a bowl. He watched, fascinated, as she added cocoa and then began scooping out an obscene amount of butter to add to the ingredients.

Yes, he could freeze them, and have them for when she was gone. He swallowed the last taste of the cupcake and realized that in just a very few short days she—and Nell—had brought some much-needed sound and life into his usually quiet house.

"I have a better idea. Not that I'm any big social butterfly, but the woman who was here cleaning my house last week mentioned that some teens from an after-school program go to Butterfly House to do yard care and odd jobs."

She paused while measuring vanilla into a spoon. "What's Butterfly House?"

He gazed longingly at the cupcakes but resisted. He didn't trust her not to give his hand a slap with the spoon she was holding. "It's a women's shelter in town. Clara—Ty's wife? She was a resident there before they were married. Ty's sister-in-law runs it."

"You're friends with the Diamonds."

"I know them probably better than anyone else in town, but that's not saying much."

"Because you keep to yourself."

He frowned. "Well, yeah."

She was watching him closely and he started to feel a little bit like he was under a microscope. Sure, he'd told her about Jane last night, because that explained his actions toward her. The rest of his life was off-limits. He had his reasons. And a big part of it was giving himself time for wounds to heal. He wasn't actually sure they ever would, or if he even wanted them to.

"I'm thinking a group of teenagers would polish off

that batch without much trouble," he added. "I can get you the number."

"As long as I leave enough for you," she said with a sly smile as she turned back to whipping the frosting.

"Of course."

A cry came from the bedroom and they both looked toward the door. "Keep doing what you're doing, I'll get her," he offered.

He picked Nell up from the bottom of the playpen and settled her in the crook of his arm. "Hey there," he said, still unused to the feel of her in his arms, not to mention the odd catch in his chest that seemed to grab him now that he acknowledged she was his flesh and blood.

"Bah, bah," Nell said, patting his face with her hand.

"Bah, bah to you, too," he answered, curling his fingers around her tiny hand and lifting it to his lips. He kissed it and then swallowed thickly. "Let's see if I can manage a diaper change," he said to her. It took him ten minutes and a few fumbles, but eventually he had her dry and happy with her soft cotton sleepers snapped up correctly.

Once upon a time he'd wanted this. He'd been close enough he could taste it and then it had been ripped away. When Jane had told him the truth she hadn't just let him go but she'd taken his hopes for the future with her. Now it was all within his grasp again. Except it wasn't, not really. When he'd thought of being a dad, he'd pictured the whole enchilada. Not trying to parent from across the country.

And after the IED accident, he'd given up on ever having a family of his own. He certainly didn't deserve it after the way he'd selfishly deserted his comrades.

But that didn't matter now, when Nell was right in front of him. "All right, Nell-bell, let's go see what your mama's up to," he suggested, and together they made their way to the kitchen.

* * *

Avery slid the cake pans into the oven, and while she was waiting used a simple plastic baggie and cut away the corner in order to pipe swirls of buttercream along the tops of the cupcakes. She was missing some crucial equipment—electric beaters would have been nice, not to mention some real decorating bags and tips, but she made do. Callum's response to her cream cheese chocolate cupcakes made it all worthwhile. With a smile she rotated her arms and topped another cupcake with the soft frosting.

Well, she wasn't completely oblivious. She'd seen how he'd looked at her last night. For a moment it had been like the way he'd looked at Crystal all those months ago. With appreciation. With...hunger. Like if either of them had leaned forward just a little he might have kissed her.

"Hey." His voice came from behind her.

She turned around and something profound stirred in her chest. He was standing in the doorway to the kitchen, Nell cushioned along the inside of his elbow, looking slightly awkward but most importantly, he was trying. There'd been such a change in him since the scene at the gas station. When she'd arrived he'd been a closed-minded, hostile stranger. Now he seemed to be thawing, showing her a kinder, more open side. What Avery hadn't been prepared for was how right it looked for him to have Nell in his arms. And how much that scared her.

"You want to try a bottle again, or did last night's remake of *The Exorcist* scare you off?" she asked.

He chuckled. "I can try again."

He was a brave one. Wordlessly she opened a can of formula and prepared a bottle. "This time," she suggested, "try putting a receiving blanket over your shoulder to save your clothes. Just in case." She reached around him and plucked a soft flannel square covered with yellow ducks from the back of a chair.

"Good idea."

They disappeared into the living room and Avery, slightly uneasy with the change in dynamic in the house, went back to focusing on her cupcakes. When the last one was frosted, she stepped back and assessed the cakes lined up on the counter. It had only been a week, but she'd missed this. Satisfied, she put the messy dishes in the sink, took her layer cake out of the oven and went to check on Nell and Callum.

Nell's eyes were wide and content even though she'd already finished with her bottle. She was happy just to lie in Callum's strong arms. Maybe that was because Callum was, for the first time, truly and completely relaxed. Avery indulged in a tender smile as she looked down at his sleeping face. Not severe like normal, and even when he smiled he often had a pinched look, as if it pained him. Now the crinkles from around his eyes were gone and so was the tightness in his jaw and lips. The image of him laughing last night came back to her, making a warmth spread through her body. When Callum forgot to be broody, he was very nearly irresistible.

And now he was so tired he was napping in the middle of the day. She knew the feeling. He was waking at night, unused to hearing a baby cry, and when he got up at five there was no going back to bed for him like there was for her.

She tiptoed from the room and went to clean up the dishes. She'd wait until Nell started to fuss and then she'd collect her. For now she'd enjoy the tiny reprieve.

Besides, the picture of Callum and Nell curled up together was too sweet to disturb.

Suddenly she had an idea. Callum would want a picture,

wouldn't he? She grabbed her phone from her purse and hurriedly clicked a photo of the two of them.

That way he'd have it when she and Nell were back in Ontario.

She tucked the phone back into her purse. He was her father and he would get a picture. She was Nell's aunt and she got her 24/7. She couldn't shake the feeling that it somehow wasn't fair. And yet the thought of giving Nell up was heartbreaking.

She couldn't do it. She just hoped that Callum stayed as reasonable about custody as he seemed to be right now.

Callum woke slowly, aware of a damp spot on his shirt and a kink in his neck. Nell was curled up on his chest, her lashes sweeping the tops of her cheeks as she slept, her lips slightly open. The more he looked at her the more he saw the family resemblance. He still remembered what his sister, Taylor, had looked like when she was born, all soft dark curls and rose-and-cream skin. His brother, Jack, too. Thinking about their childhood made him feel a bit homesick. He hadn't spoken to his siblings in months.

There was no doubt that Nell was his. The question now was, what was he going to do about it?

He had no answer. It was still too new. Too...confusing. How could you raise a child from thousands of kilometers away?

As he sat in the chair he realized there was a new scent in the air, something very different from the chocolate of earlier—something rich and spicy that made his mouth water. Music was playing softly on the radio he kept in the kitchen and he paused, listening. Sure enough, Avery was singing along—she didn't have a bad voice, really—and it sounded like she was keeping the beat with some sort of utensil. Stifling a smile, he pushed himself up from the chair, careful not to wake Nell, and stepped to the doorway of the kitchen.

His gaze was drawn immediately to Avery, standing at the stove with a spoon in her hand. Her back was to him and something hot flickered through him as she moved her hips to the beat of the song. The spoon went round in circles in the pan and her blond ponytail bobbed as she hummed with the verse. But as soon as the chorus came on again her hips started the same subtle gyration.

She had perfect rhythm. And the perfect bottom to display it.

He cleared his throat.

The spoon flew up in her hand as she spun around, startled. Reddish sauce flew off the end and spattered on the wall next to the stove. "You scared me to death!" she exclaimed, her eyes wide. Then she reached for a cloth and hurried to wipe the sauce away. "I didn't hear you come in."

"Clearly. You had your groove on."

She blushed. Up her neck, over her cheeks, right to the roots of her hair.

He stepped forward. "What's that? It smells great."

"Oh." She gathered herself together and smiled. "Spicy Peanut Chicken and Basmati."

It sounded a bit exotic to his tastes but he wasn't a picky eater and he liked anything with kick. "I could smell it as soon as I woke up."

"There's dessert, too, so that you'll keep your hands off my cupcakes." She nodded toward the other end of the counter where a layer cake sat on a plate. "Lemon chiffon with buttercream and coconut."

She'd had time to bake a cake, too? "How long was I asleep?"

She laughed. "It's nearly six. Nell fell back asleep, too. She'll probably be up all night."

Six? When had he last napped like that?

He looked at her latest creation. She hadn't just slapped on the buttercream. She'd smoothed it around the sides and on top, and then piped more of the icing around the base in little rosettes. All along the top she'd made five-petaled flowers, each with a little yellow candy in the middle, and she'd dusted the inside of the flower circlet with snowy coconut.

It wasn't cake. It was art.

"I couldn't find a lot of supplies in town, so I made do. What do you think?"

What he thought was that if she could do something this beautiful without her regular tools, she must be amazing when she had her whole arsenal at her disposal.

"It looks great," he said. At her crestfallen expression he realized the compliment had been pretty lackluster. "It's beautiful, Avery. You're obviously very good at what you do."

She waved a hand at him. "Go, wash up and get ready. We can just put Nell in her seat until she wakes up."

It felt increasingly strange, sharing a table with her. Like…like a family. He hadn't had that feeling in a really long time nor did he want to get used to it. It wasn't something he thought he deserved nor did he trust it. He'd played house once before. Thought he'd had it all. He'd been so wrong.

He looked over at Avery, at Nell, tasted the spicy chicken and fragrant rice in his mouth and reminded himself that Avery was not his. And biology aside, neither was Nell. She belonged with Avery. A baby needed a mother. No matter what came of these few weeks, he was certain of that single fact.

When the main dish was cleared away she cut him a huge slab of cake and brought it to him with a glass of cold milk.

The first taste was pure heaven.

The second was even better.

And by the time he had his third, he knew going back to dry sandwiches and store-bought cookies was going to be hell.

Nell awakened as he finished every last crumb, and he watched Avery pour something out of a box into a tiny bowl. She added warm milk from Nell's bottle and stirred it up, and then she took out the smallest spoon he'd ever seen and put just a bit of the mixture on the tip.

"What are you doing?"

"Oh, Clara suggested I try Nell on a little cereal in the evenings. Just a teaspoon or so. She's almost five months old now. I was going to wait for six, but Clara said a little rice cereal might do the trick to getting her to sleep through the night. Though after that nap, it might be a while before she's ready for bed." She touched the spoon to the baby's lips and Nell smacked a bit, trying it out, sticking out her tongue. Avery laughed as each little spoonful seemed to end up either smeared on Nell's face or on her bib. But soon the teaspoon of cereal was gone and she was wiping Nell's face with a warm cloth.

"Aren't you having any cake?"

"Once she's had her bottle and bath."

"Oh."

Avery picked up Nell and grabbed the bottle before heading to the living room.

"Avery?" Callum made himself stay in his chair rather than follow.

"Yes?" she called, and he heard the creak of the chair.

"Thanks for dinner," he answered back.

"You're welcome," she said, and he heard the rhythmic sound of his La-Z-Boy rocking back and forth.

He got up from the table and resisted the urge to follow her, to look at her rocking his daughter.

His daughter.

And there it was. That panic again at the very thought. How could he have a child in this world? The world was ugly and flawed. He had no right having children. Jane had at least been right about that.

So he made himself busy putting dishes in the dishwasher. Anything to help him keep his distance. Because Avery and Nell were getting close.

Too close. They made him forget all sorts of things that he needed to remember forever.

Ever since he'd stepped into the kitchen and caught sight of her hips keeping time with the radio, there'd been something else. He'd been tempted to go up behind her and place his hands on her hips, maybe lean forward and whisper something in her ear.

Which was, of course, insane. Of course he hadn't acted on the impulse. He was rather uncomfortable that he'd had the urge in the first place. Not just now, either. Last night, on the porch. Maybe even before then, like that first day when they'd collided in the hall. It hadn't only been thoughts of Nell keeping him up at night.

The sound of the baby's cries echoing through the house was strange, but what was really odd was that it wasn't exactly unpleasant. Last night it had been 12:42 a.m. He knew because he'd been lying in bed awake, thinking about Avery's red lips and their confessions in the dark. He'd heard the thin cry as Nell woke, hungry, and Avery's soft voice answering her. The sounds of Avery heating a bottle in the kitchen and the creak of the floor as she put Nell back to bed.

He'd gone to sleep after that, but it had been restless, leaving him feeling even more tired this morning.

It wasn't just Nell he had to worry about. It was Avery, and all the uncomfortable feelings she spawned just by being her normal, giving self.

He'd given up wishing long ago. He hadn't expected to feel these sorts of emotions again, and he both loved her and hated her for making him remember—and hope—when he knew exactly how it all would end.

CHAPTER EIGHT

Butterfly House was a rambling, old-fashioned house painted a restful yellow with white trim. A veranda graced the front, the steps flanked on either side by pots of geraniums and purply-blue lobelia. Avery liked it on sight.

Callum put the truck in Park on the street outside the house. "Do you want me to wait?"

"I know you've got work, so I can just drop them off."

"Or you can stay. I have to go to the hardware store for some supplies to fix the east gate. I can swing by and pick you up on the way back."

"What about Nell?"

She glimpsed a moment of consternation. If he'd asked, she'd have let him take Nell shopping with him. But Callum was intensely private. At home was one thing, but out about town was another. The last thing he'd want would be taking an infant to a public shop, opening himself up to all sorts of speculation.

"I'll bring her in," he offered.

So together they made their way up the walk to the house, Avery with her hands full of treats and Callum with the handle of the car seat in his strong hand. He rang the bell and stepped back, and within moments the door opened.

"Hi, you must be Avery." A pretty woman with long

dark hair that was pulled back in a ponytail smiled at her. "I'm Angela Diamond. We spoke on the phone. Come on in."

"Thanks. Hope you don't mind I brought a plus one." Avery stepped aside to reveal the car seat and Callum.

"Hi, Callum," Angela greeted. "Good to see you. And who have we here? Oh, my, aren't you precious!" Angela looked up at Avery. "She's just a little older than my little guy, Ryan," she said. "He's almost eight weeks."

"Congratulations," Avery offered. She turned to look at Callum. "We're okay now. I'll see you in a little bit?"

"I shouldn't be more than half an hour or so."

"Perfect."

Callum jogged down the steps and started the truck. When he was gone, Avery relaxed and smiled at Angela. "Let's get these inside before the frosting melts."

"Good idea." Angela took the cupcakes and Avery grabbed the seat. They walked through to the large kitchen and Angela put the containers on an island. "Hang on a minute. Ryan's probably awake by now and they can say hello."

Avery took Nell out of the seat and balanced her on her hip, looking around the room. Cozy, warm, with a huge kitchen table that seated at least eight. Considering close to half a dozen women lived here, the place was absolutely spotless. When Angela came back with Ryan in her arms, Avery said as much.

"It's so quiet…and clean."

Angela laughed. "We have a chore list. Everyone has their own responsibilities to keep things ship-shape."

"Callum didn't tell me much about what you do." She smiled down at the tiny bundle in Angela's arms. Not long ago Nell had been that small. "And he's adorable, by the way."

"We think so. Though I could use a little more sleep."

"I hear you." Avery relaxed, noticed Angela's hips were rocking back and forth instinctively in a soothing motion. It was neat to be talking with another mom, someone with a baby so close in age to Nell. It wasn't something Avery had experienced much. Her boss's kids were teens now and most of the girls at the bakery were still single or dating.

"Butterfly House is kind of a step-up home where victims of abuse get ready to start a new chapter in their lives. We help with housing, employment counseling, budgeting…that sort of thing. The kids will be along soon to mow the grass and do the weeding and stuff," Angela continued. "During the summer the after-school program in the area kind of drops off. This gives some of those kids a place to be, even if it's only for an afternoon a week. We get our yard work done and my contribution is snacks. Well," she amended, "not *my* contribution. I oversee the whole foundation now, and we have a local director. She's got the day off today, so I'm here instead. And you've kindly provided the snacks."

Avery grinned. "Honestly I was going a little stir-crazy out at Callum's. It felt good to bake again, but the problem is finding enough bodies to eat it. I'm used to baking dozens at a time where I work."

Angela's gaze turned speculative as she reached for a cupcake, keeping it away from Ryan's curious fingers. "So, you and Callum. What's that about?"

Avery deliberated and then figured the truth was probably easiest. And Callum trusted the Diamond family, which she knew was a big thing for him. He had to have known there would be questions today—and trusted her to give the answers.

Hmm. She hadn't quite thought of it that way before.

He trusted her. Considering how their relationship began, it was a nice feeling.

"Callum is Nell's father," she said simply. "And my niece. We're just figuring everything out for now."

"He's a pretty private guy."

"No kidding." Avery smiled. "Private, stubborn…"

"…strong and handsome…" Angela continued, smiling.

Avery flushed. "It's not like that."

"Are you sure? I was positive I sensed something between you before he left."

A little jolt ran through Avery at the observation. It was bad enough that she felt this sizzle of chemistry whenever she was with Callum, but heavens, was it noticeable to everyone else, too?

"I'm sure," she lied, swallowing hard. "Here, why don't you try one?"

Angela took the bait and accepted a cake. "Oh, my gosh, this is delicious."

"Thanks."

"This is what you do? You're a baker?"

Avery nodded. "I do cakes and cupcakes for a bakery back in Ontario. I get the precision of following a recipe with the creativity of decorating and developing new flavors."

"These really are good." She bit into the cream cheese filling and closed her eyes. "Hey, you've met my sister-in-law Clara, right?"

Avery recalled the bubbly blonde who was Angela's sister-in-law. "Yes, we met at Callum's."

"Clara was my first resident here. That first summer, she and some of the women had a chili cook-off at the Cadence Creek Rodeo, and it's become an annual event. It's coming up next weekend. We're planning on using it as a fundraiser for the foundation, but it would be awesome if we had something a little different. How do you feel about making some special cupcakes for the tent?"

Avery thought Angela might be reading more into her involvement with Callum than she should. The last thing Avery wanted was to get too involved with either Callum or the town—nice as it seemed to be.

On the other hand, it was a good cause, and a chance to do what she did best.

"You did say you were bored," Angela offered, an innocent expression on her face.

"How many are we talking?" Avery asked. "Seven, eight dozen?"

"Oh, at least that many. Big men, big eaters around here. What do you say, are you in? If not, I guess I could hit up the girls at the bakery in town, but they're usually pretty busy."

And completely unimaginative. Avery would never say so and insult Callum's neighbors but it was true. Already she was picturing something neat in her mind, something new she hadn't done before. This was her favorite part of her job—coming up with something fresh and fun.

"Does everyone in town go to these things?" she asked.

"Pretty much, at one point or another during the weekend. It's the main event for the summer in Cadence Creek, other than Canada Day and the parade. Friday night there's opening ceremonies, then all day Saturday is the rodeo and fireworks after dark. Then on Sunday afternoon it's the rodeo finals."

It all sounded like a lot of fun, and Avery had never been to a rodeo before. Plus it would give her something to occupy her time—and maybe think a little less about Callum. "You've got a deal. Just tell me when and where to deliver them."

"I'll call you midweek with the final details. Thanks

so much for helping out." There was a knock at the door and Angela grinned. "Looks like the crew's here. What do you think, cupcakes before work or after?"

The house got loud and busy as half a dozen teens came in, chatting and laughing. As Angela gave them instructions, Callum drove up and—to her surprise—came to the door to fetch her.

"I'll see you next Saturday," Angela called after her with a wave.

Callum took the car seat from Avery's hands. "What's that about?"

Avery fought against the feeling that this all seemed so normal. It wasn't. She was still a guest. She was not part of this town. She knew where she belonged and it wasn't here.

But why shouldn't she enjoy herself in the meantime?

"Oh, I agreed to make some cupcakes for the foundation fundraiser next weekend. I hear the rodeo's in town."

Callum paused by the truck. "You want to go to that?"

She shrugged. "I've never been to a rodeo before. It might be fun."

"It'll be hot as Hades. And what about Nell?"

Belatedly she realized she might be putting Callum in an awkward position, especially as he remained oddly silent. "Oh," she said quietly. "Of course. I never thought… it's rather public, isn't it?" And despite this morning, obviously he didn't want to appear as a family to the town in general.

He opened the door to the truck. "A bit," he answered.

Her bubble of excitement popped. Well, she could still do the baking. It just meant that she would take the cupcakes to the grounds and drop them off, that's all. She was disappointed, but she understood that Callum kept things private. It had all happened so fast; there was bound to be awkward questions. Explaining the situation could be both difficult and uncomfortable for him. He probably wasn't even planning on going at all.

They drove home through the summer afternoon with only the radio providing any noise inside the truck cab.

And when they got home, Callum took off for the barn and afternoon chores, leaving Avery and Nell to fend for themselves.

It was nearly dark when Callum made his way inside. No lights were on and he wondered briefly if Avery had already put Nell to bed.

He'd been hiding out in the barn, plain and simple, using the exertion of physical labor to try to banish the odd feeling in his heart. He knew that feeling and he didn't want it. It was hope. It was, he'd realized with quite a start, happiness. All because of the simple mention of Avery making stupid cupcakes for next week's rodeo, like she was already a part of this town and a part of his life.

She wasn't. And the ache, the hope, all of it, had hit him like a ton of bricks because he'd suddenly realized that on some level he was going to miss her when she left. Not just Nell, but Avery, too. Her smile, her pretty eyes, the way her cheeks flushed when he looked at her a few seconds too long.

And that was frustrating because he'd never wanted to feel those sorts of emotions again.

But it was hardly her fault, was it? Instead he'd discouraged her and run off without another word. Like a coward.

His eyes adjusted to the darkness as he stepped inside the living room and realized she was sitting on the sofa, Nell cradled in her arms. Her eyes glowed at him in the pale light, still wide-awake despite the late hour. Still with the power to hit him square in the gut with their honesty.

"You're still up," he said, his voice low.

"She fell asleep a while ago, but we were so comfortable I didn't want to get up."

"Not brooding in the dark?"

He saw her lashes blink. "That's more your style, isn't it?"

"Yes," he admitted, and the confession took the sting out of the words.

He went to the room and perched on the arm of the wing chair. "I'm sorry I disappeared."

"You could have spent time with her tonight," Avery pressed. She wasn't letting him off easily, and that was one of the things he truly liked about her. He knew he wasn't an easy man to be around, but she didn't let him get away with his moodiness. And she was right. He'd missed out on time with Nell. Truth be told, he'd also missed out on time with Avery. Which was probably good considering the direction of his thoughts, but unfortunately she and Nell seemed to be a package deal.

"I know. Could I take her in to bed?"

"I suppose."

He'd washed up at the sink in the barn and so he went straight to her. Carefully he moved to take the baby, but when he did the backs of his fingers slid along the inside of her arm, skimming dangerously close to the side of her breast.

He swallowed tightly as he paused, then came to his senses. As gently as possible he lifted Nell into his arms…a feeling that was growing more natural each time he did it. It was hard to believe he was just getting used to her and she'd soon be gone. How much would she change until he saw her again? Would she be walking? Talking? She certainly wouldn't remember who he was…

He placed her in bed and pulled up the light covers,

staring down at her for a few minutes. Ontario to Alberta was no way to run a family.

But this wasn't a family unit, was it? It was coparenting, a whole different dynamic. And he was completely at sea—with his feelings about being a dad, for Nell—even what he felt for Avery.

She was still sitting on the sofa when he went back out to the living room. He reached for a lamp on the end table but her soft voice stopped him. "Leave it," she said in a light whisper.

He pulled his hand back.

"You want to sit in the dark?"

He barely saw the tiny nod. "It's quiet," she said, "and peaceful."

And intimate. That didn't escape him, either. He should probably leave her be and get out of there. Instead he found himself asking, "Do you mind if I sit with you?"

"Of course not." He heard the slight hesitation anyway and felt guilty for interrupting her privacy. But there were things he felt he should say. Sorry, for one.

Callum perched on the sofa cushion beside her and braced his elbows on his knees, linking his hands loosely in front of him. "I'm sorry for my reaction this afternoon," he said. "If you want to go to the rodeo, you should go. I don't want to stand in your way."

"I understand your need for privacy," she murmured. "Really, I do."

"It's not that." It was, but not entirely. It had more to do with how he chose to live than people finding out he had a daughter. He liked to keep his demons to himself.

"I'm not ashamed of Nell, Avery. I want you to know that right off the bat."

She turned a little, putting her knees closer to his thighs. "But?"

"But going there…together…"

"You're worried people will get the wrong idea."

Her voice was flat and he closed his eyes, trying to find the right way to say what he needed to. "Not the wrong idea. There are things about me I just don't want people to know, so I keep to myself." He sighed. "Whatever is, or isn't, going on isn't anyone's business but ours."

"What *is* going on?" she asked.

And just like that the air in the room changed, grew heavier, charged.

"Avery…"

He shouldn't have said her name. It hovered between them, full of unspoken possibilities.

"There's something," she murmured. "I see it when you look at me. I don't know what to do about it."

"God." He exhaled sharply. He hadn't expected her to come right out with it, not after the way they'd been tap-dancing around each other the whole visit.

"It's not just me then, right?"

He didn't want this. Didn't want to have feelings at all. It was better to stay dead inside, avoid all the pain that came from disappointing people. From losing them. He considered lying to her, denying that he was in any way attracted to her. But maybe they needed to get it out in the open. Deal with it and put it behind them. "It's not just you," he confessed.

The tension multiplied, humming between them.

He swallowed. "It's awkward considering the circumstances. I mean…Crystal…"

She seemed terribly close to him on the sofa. Close enough he could reach out and touch her if he wanted. She smelled like baby powder and some sort of fresh floral scent that drove him crazy.

"Of course," she said, her voice resigned. "I've never quite been able to measure up to Crystal."

That wasn't what he'd meant, but he could see that was how she'd taken it. She'd made a few similar remarks during her time here, giving him the impression that she considered herself somehow lacking in comparison to her sister when it couldn't be further from the truth. "That's not it at all. Just…don't you kind of find it weird? That I…" He hesitated. Choosing the right words was so important and he was stumbling over everything.

"That you slept with my sister?"

It sounded horrible when she put it like that.

"Callum," she finally said, when he remained silent. "She's gone. None of it matters anymore."

He wanted to believe that. And yet he knew that she still felt the differences between herself and Crystal. And she shouldn't.

"Just because you are different than Crystal doesn't mean you are any less attractive. You're just as beautiful as she was, just in a different way. A quieter way."

In a way that was the difference between a weekend fling and a lifetime. In a way that went far beyond skin-deep and right into the heart of her. He knew what it was like to feel ugly. Unworthy. There were good reasons for him to feel that way. But not her. She was the most honorable, unselfish woman he'd ever met.

"You're the most amazing person I know," he said quietly, but when he looked into her shadowed face he saw the glimmer of tears on her cheeks.

Shaken, he reached out to wipe them away. Her cheek was warm beneath the pad of his thumb and for a second he held his breath.

He knew he shouldn't be touching her. Knew it would confuse everything and mix it up. And yet he couldn't seem to stop himself from easing forward, closing the distance between them. Her hand touched his forearm and her fingers tightened on his skin.

"Callum," she said, a little breathlessly. The simple sound of his name on her lips toppled him over the edge of what was prudent. He could see her eyes clearly now, glowing at him in the darkness of the moonlit room, could see the full curve of her lips as they parted slightly, heard the way her breath seemed to hitch and her lashes fluttered shut as he closed the gap between them…

And then he touched his lips to hers.

Avery's heart pounded what felt like double-time, which was disturbing since her lungs seemed unable to get enough air. Callum's gaze held hers as he leaned closer and she felt herself moving to meet him. They shouldn't do this. It would be a horrible mistake to make the situation more complicated than it already was.

But he was here, and he was strong and masculine and handsome and he'd called her beautiful and amazing and how was a girl supposed to have any defenses at the end of all that?

Besides, she really, really wanted to know what it was to kiss him. If his lips were as warm and soft as they looked. If the sexy stubble that always seemed to shadow his jaw was rough or soft.

Her lashes fluttered to her cheeks by sheer instinct as her fingers dug into his muscled forearm.

The first contact was soft, a featherlight test that left her hungry for more. She leaned forward and pressed her mouth more firmly to his. His body tensed beneath her fingers and she realized that he was holding back. She didn't want him to. Just once she wanted to feel like the subject of unbridled passion. Like a man was dying of thirst and she was cool, lifesaving water. She slid her hand from his forearm over to the hard, warm wall of his chest. His heart beat through the soft cotton, hammering against her palm. For a moment their lips parted and the only sound was the rush of their breathing as decision hung in the balance.

"I shouldn't," he whispered. "We shouldn't."

But she twisted her fingers in his T-shirt and held on. "I'm so tired of being the responsible one. The good one. The boring one," she confessed. Whispering in the dark added to the sense of excitement. It almost felt...illicit. "Please, Callum. We don't have to go any further than this. Just kiss me again, please."

She'd set the boundary, had taken the unusual step of actually asking for what she wanted. Would he give it to her, or would he walk away?

Could she bear the humiliation if he turned her away?

His lips touched the soft skin of the outside of her ear. "Never boring," he murmured, sending chills down her spine.

"Show me," she suggested, surprised at herself for voicing her wants so easily.

His hand curled around the back of her neck, firm and warm as their breath mingled. "You're sure?" he asked, the words low and inviting.

She nodded a little.

His mouth met hers again, firmer, more demanding and desire spiraled through her belly straight to her core. Her pulse raced as he opened his mouth wider. Her hand slid up and tangled in his hair, fisting in the long strands. It was surprisingly soft, the whole sensation foreign from anything she'd ever experienced before.

And yet he was true to his word. He didn't try to push her down into the cushions of the couch or take things further than a kiss. She was as disappointed as she was relieved.

His lips slid past the corner of her mouth and over her cheek. "We've got to stop," he warned. "I have to stop."

"Are you sure?" she breathed, echoing his earlier words. She didn't want him to pull away. He felt too good, too right.

"I'm sure." His voice was firmer now in the dark. She ran her hand over his nape and he shivered against her fingers. "Avery. If we don't stop now I'm not going to want to stop at all."

"So?"

Good heavens, where had this bravery come from? Normally so cautious, so careful. Everything well thought out. Yet right now she was prepared to throw caution to the wind for a night in Callum's bed.

"There's a little girl in there who needs us to keep this uncomplicated. A kiss is one thing. Making love…"

Avery's breath caught. Not just having sex. He'd used the words *making love,* which was a whole lot different. And he was right. She swallowed and let out her breath. "It would look different in the clear light of day."

"Walking away from a kiss is very different than walking away after spending the night together," he said.

"Yet you did it with Crystal." She said the words and could have bitten her tongue once they were out. Why, oh, why, did she feel compelled to keep bringing that up?

"Crystal wasn't you," he answered simply.

She was dying to know what that meant—and too afraid to ask. She slid back on the sofa, putting inches between them. "Well, I guess we satisfied our curiosity anyway." She tried to inject a lightness in her voice that she didn't feel.

A sardonic chuckle sounded in the dark. "Not nearly.

But it's for the best. Soon you'll be going back to Ontario. No need to make things more difficult than they need to be."

Did that mean he was going to miss her? It couldn't possibly. She just hoped that he would miss Nell. And that what he meant was that there was no sense in making things weirder between them in the meantime.

"I should probably go to bed now. It's late."

"Yes, it is."

"You must be tired." She realized quite belatedly that he hadn't even eaten any dinner.

"I'll be along in a bit," he said.

She got up, found her knees a bit wobbly. "I guess I'll see you in the morning, then," she offered weakly. "Good night."

"Night," he replied.

When Avery finished brushing her teeth and came out of the bathroom, he was still sitting in the same spot.

And she was staring at the ceiling a long time later when she heard him finally get up and make his way down the hall to his bedroom.

As Avery cracked eggs into the frying pan, she realized how very right Callum had been to shut things down last night.

Right now he was behind her, playing with Nell while Avery made breakfast. There'd been an awkward pause first thing when he'd entered the kitchen, but then he'd covered it and simply said good morning before turning his attention to his daughter.

His daughter. That was what Avery had conveniently put to the back of her mind last night when it had been dark and late and he'd been far too tempting.

A shout came from behind her and she spun, spatula in

hand, to find Nell in Callum's arms, her tiny fingers fisted in his hair. His head was at an odd angle because she was yanking on it. Nell seemed totally unconcerned.

Avery's hand flew to her mouth as she laughed. "And now you understand why I wear ponytails most of the time."

With one hand he untangled his hair from Nell's grip. When he looked up his eyes had watered and Avery laughed again.

"I suppose I should see a barber. I've let it go for far too long." He put Nell back in her seat and buckled the clips to keep her from scooting out.

She wondered why he'd neglected cutting his hair. Granted, his house had been a bit of a disaster when she'd arrived, but from what she could see of his farm and equipment, he kept things neat and in tip-top shape. Maybe it was all part of his recluse act—an act she was starting to see through more each day.

"I could cut it for you if you have a good pair of scissors," she offered.

"You could?" He raised one skeptical eyebrow. "I know you can make cupcakes and probably have other talents, but I'm not sure I want to be your guinea pig when it comes to haircuts."

"Suit yourself. You can always drive into town to the barber shop—you do have one, right? Or I think I saw a salon on Main Street somewhere. The ladies there would probably throw in a head massage," she teased.

Truthfully she'd gotten used to the longer look, especially after tangling her fingers in it last night. Heat rose to her cheeks and she turned back to flip the eggs.

"It's just hair. I could let you have a go at it and save myself the twenty bucks. Of course if you ruin it, I can always get it shaved off in town. I haven't had the army look for a while."

"Why'd you leave the forces, anyway?" Avery was glad for a change of subject, giving her something else to focus on. "From what I gathered, you were itching to get back after Pete's wedding."

He was so quiet that she frowned and turned back around. He was staring out the kitchen window, his shoulders tensed.

"Did I say something wrong?"

He shrugged and turned back, but the tight expression on his face reminded her of the first day when he'd opened the door to find her standing on his step. He'd loosened up a lot since then, but whatever had prompted him to lock himself away here hadn't gone away. She'd initially figured it was Jane and how she'd broken his heart. But now she wondered if it was something more.

"Let's just say I left before they could kick me out," he replied. "Those eggs ready yet?"

He reached for a plate on the counter but she pulled it out of reaching distance. "Why would they have kicked you out?"

He frowned, looking surprised she was holding his plate hostage and annoyed at her question. "The eggs are going to burn."

"I turned off the heat." She raised her eyebrows, waiting for an answer.

He sighed. "Fine. Let's just say I had a bit of a problem with authority when I went back on that last deployment."

"You? Mr. Straight and Narrow?"

He held out his hand for the plate. She put two eggs on it, added a few strips of bacon and gave it to him.

In return he gave her one more tidbit. "I was angry all

the time. About Jane, about the baby. About life. I mouthed off a little too often to the wrong person."

"What happened?"

He sat down at the table and cut across an egg with the side of his fork, popped the piece in his mouth and chewed. "Good eggs," he said, reaching for his coffee. Avoiding her eyes.

Message received. She'd gotten as much out of him as she was going to today.

She sat down across from him and nibbled at her breakfast but in the silence she was transported back to last night on the couch in the gray light of the living room. Hearing him say a kiss was easier to walk away from than making love.

He was a complicated man. He was her niece's father, for heaven's sake! And a man she was going to be connected to for years to come. He was right. Going to bed with him would have been a mistake—not to mention completely out of character for her.

All the rationale in the world didn't stop the wanting, though. And neither did the daylight.

He finished his meal in record time and took his plate to the sink. "I'll take you up on your haircut offer this evening, if it still holds," he said, stopping by the doorway to the kitchen.

"It does." Swallowing, she gathered the courage to ask him a favor. "Callum, do you think I could borrow your truck again today? I have an idea for the Butterfly House cupcakes but I can't get the materials here in Cadence Creek."

He frowned. "I could probably take you, if you can wait a few hours."

"But you must have stuff to do here. I don't want to

take you away from work. I probably should have kept the rental…"

"I don't mind you using the truck. But are you sure you can park that beast?"

She nodded. "From what I gather, there's tons of parking and it shouldn't be too busy on a weekday. I've driven our bakery delivery truck before. I'm sure I'll be fine, as long as you don't need it."

"Then go ahead. I don't need to use it today."

"Thanks, Callum."

He was just about ready to leave when she added, "Is there anything you need in Edmonton?"

"Not that I can think of."

"I'll have my cell. You can call me if you think of anything."

"Okay." He took the keys out of his pocket and put them on the counter. "Drive safe," he said, before leaving the kitchen and heading back outside.

That had been remarkably easy, she realized. It was a shock to realize he trusted her. It wasn't just a truck, it was his main farm vehicle, too.

In just a matter of days their lives had managed to intertwine in small and subtle ways.

Going back to her quiet apartment suddenly seemed more of a letdown than something she was looking forward to.

CHAPTER NINE

THE TOWEL WAS wrapped around Callum's neck and he closed his eyes as Avery pulled the comb through his hair. She'd suggested he wet it first and then shower later to wash off any pieces of hair not collected by the towel-cape. Over and over she combed through the long strands, getting out any tangles before starting to use the scissors. It felt wonderful.

Why had he let it get this long? He finally admitted to himself that it was about turning his back on his old life. If the old Callum shaved his head and said *Yes, sir*, the new Callum would be completely different. He'd wear his hair however he damn well pleased and he'd be his own boss, thank you very much. In control of his own life and destiny.

Until, of course, Avery had shown up with Nell. Suddenly he wasn't the only person who mattered most. Avery had no idea that this was about more than a haircut. It was letting go of the one thing that had kept him going since coming back from deployment. Being totally different and in charge.

"You ready?"

He nodded.

The first snip of scissors and a chunk of hair dropped to the floor. Another, and another, until the chair was surrounded by the dark strands. Her hands felt wonderful running over his scalp, the snip-snip of the scissors hypnotic as she moved to one side, then the other. She stepped in front of him and worked on the front, his gaze level with her breasts and he swallowed. Last night he'd done the right thing by walking away. Didn't mean he didn't go to bed and think about what might have happened.

He held perfectly still as she shaped the hair around his ears and along the back of his neck, the blades of the scissors cool against his skin. Finally she stepped back. "I think that's it. Go tell me what you think."

He got up carefully, shaking out any extra hair onto the floor, then went to the bathroom to look in the mirror. It surprised him to see his face so clearly. She'd done a good job. One sideburn was slightly longer than the other, but he could fix that when he shaved with a quick flick of the razor. It wasn't long, but it wasn't military-short, either. It was somewhere in between and he kind of liked it.

"Is it okay?" She'd come up behind him silently and he turned away from the image in the mirror.

"It's great. It'll be a lot cooler for sure."

"And no baby-pulling," Avery added with a smile.

"Definitely a bonus."

His gaze met hers and she stared at him for a long moment. "What?" he asked.

"Oh." She laughed a little. "Nothing. I'd better go get this swept up."

While she went back to the kitchen to sweep up the hair, he turned on the shower. The back of his neck was starting to itch and he figured he'd better get the extra hair washed off before it drove him crazy.

When he came back out of the bathroom, he heard her humming in the kitchen as dishes clattered. There was the shake of the rattle beating an off-time percussion to the tune and he stopped, his heart in his throat.

This was what he'd always wanted. What he'd thought he'd have—what he'd almost had with Jane. Home and family. A wife and a baby, regular everyday sounds that probably seemed mundane to anyone else but meant so much to him. He'd always had that at home—parents that had stuck together and his brother and sister to look out for. It wasn't until he was grown that he realized how very rare it was for a marriage to last like theirs had. Or how lonely it would be to almost have it and lose it from right beneath his nose.

He was fooling himself with Avery. One kiss didn't mean much in the big scheme of things. She was leaving and going home in a matter of days. And there was no way in hell he was going to make a fool of himself by trying for something more only to get a slap in the face. Her life was there. Her job—the job she loved—was there. She wasn't about to give it up for some small-potatoes dairy farmer in this sleepy small town.

But if time was running out with her, it was also running out with Nell, and he wanted to make the most of the days and hours left. Resolved, he stepped inside the kitchen. Avery was standing at the counter with mixing bowls and a variety of ingredients out on its surface.

"Baking?"

She grinned. "Trying out a few new recipes. I want the rodeo day to have something super special."

"Why don't I take Nell off your hands? It's a nice night. I thought I'd take her outside for a while."

Surprise widened her eyes. "That'd be fine."

He nodded. "She won't be here much longer. I need to get in all the time I can."

He reached into the seat and plucked the baby out, settling her weight at his elbow.

Avery's eyes glistened at him. "Thank you," she murmured, putting down a measuring cup. "For being so accepting and making the effort you have."

"I'm her father," he said simply. "And it's my job to do what's best for her."

He left Avery in the kitchen and headed out the door, intent on showing Nell the garden and the rosebushes and the waving fields where his cows grazed.

He'd said it was his job to do what was best for her. Trouble was, he really had no idea what that was. He was totally flying blind.

Avery let out the breath she was holding.

Callum had taken Nell outside and she could see them through the window, walking by the edge of the vegetable garden. Nell wasn't even six months old yet and he was talking to her—Avery could see his lips move—and pointing at something on a plant. Seeing his dark head next to Nell's sent something tender to her heart. She was glad he was embracing fatherhood. But it made her feel guilty to know she was going to be tearing them apart in a week's time.

She put her attention back to her batter, alternating milk and flour until it was smooth as silk. Cutting Callum's hair had been far more intimate than she'd expected. Just touching him as she measured the strands between her fingers and clipped with the scissors had put her senses on high alert. And when she'd gone to stand in front of him, and could feel the warmth of his breath flutter her blouse, it had been all she could do to stop herself from taking his face in her hands and kissing him again.

What in the world had come over her? It had been a

long time since she'd been in a relationship, but this sort of behavior, this aching need for him, was completely unlike her.

And now his hair was shorter and he looked completely different. Less dangerous, but it brought out the angle of his cheekbones and the color of his eyes, a warm, chocolaty shade that seemed to cut right into the heart of her.

For a minute she considered what would happen if she decided to move closer to Cadence Creek. He'd be able to see Nell more often, but that also meant their paths would cross frequently. As far as her apartment, well, it was home but there was no one waiting for her anymore. The true sticking point was her job. She loved it. She'd even planned on revisiting the topic of expanding The Icing on Top with Denise—with the idea that she could manage a second store once Nell was a bit older.

Now Callum's words echoed in her head. *I'm her father, and it's my job to do what's best for her.*

She was Nell's mother now, so wasn't it also her job to put Nell first? And wouldn't being closer to Callum be best for his daughter?

Somehow she'd have to find a way to put these feelings that kept cropping up to the wayside. And she definitely wasn't going to decide anything right away. If she were to move, it was a big decision and she had to make sure she had a way to support the both of them first, wherever they landed. Callum would pay child support, she knew that. But she also knew she wouldn't rely on him to support *her*. She would look after herself—and her share of Nell's expenses. She would never, ever take advantage of Callum that way, especially knowing about his past.

First she had to get this batch of cupcakes into the oven. And get the order for the rodeo out of the way.

Then maybe she could start putting out feelers—maybe

in Edmonton, or even Calgary. A few hours' drive was way better than halfway across the country, right?

She put the first pan in the oven and went to the patio door looking over the pasture. Callum was standing by a fence with Nell perched on the top wooden rail, ensconced in his arms as the sun began to set, washing everything in a peachy-orange glow.

When she'd arrived she'd wanted Callum to know the truth and for him to send them back to Burlington with his blessing. He was prepared to do that, too. She was the one who'd changed.

Because looking at the two of them together, she wasn't sure she had it in her to tear them apart.

Avery took another pan of cupcakes out of the oven and set them on top of the stove to cool before taking them out of the tin. This made four dozen, with another four to go. Just over one hundred miniature red fondant Stetsons were placed precisely on parchment paper, waiting to be perched on top of the cream cheese and chili buttercream she had yet to make.

Callum had been true to his word about spending time with Nell. Once milking and breakfast was done, he'd spend some time playing with her or taking her for a walk outside. He took her on a trip with him to the feed store, which surprised the heck out of Avery as it was rather public when all was said and done. At night he learned how to feed her cereal from the soft-tipped spoon and gave her her last bottle before bed. He'd even given her a bath when she'd had a diaper explosion during the hour that Avery had zipped off to the grocery store for more supplies.

In a matter of weeks he'd gone from outright denial to being a hands-on dad.

She relined the tin with cupcake papers and frowned.

As much as he'd taken to spending time with Nell, he'd been noticeably avoiding Avery. Nothing she could put her finger on, but he seemed careful that there was always a space between them. There definitely were no more kisses, no more accidental touches. Which was probably just as well, but Avery was disappointed just the same.

Right now he had Nell over at Diamondback Ranch—he'd gone to talk to Sam and Tyson about farm business and said it would be good for Nell to see the other children. Avery smiled to herself. Nell wasn't even mobile on her own, and neither was Sam and Angela's son, and she expected either Clara or Angela would end up having an extra baby on their hands.

But she didn't say a word about it because she didn't feel she could deny him anything when it came to Nell right now.

When they finally came back, she was putting the last swirls of buttercream on the final cupcakes. He entered the kitchen with Nell on his arm and Avery's heart gave a little kick, seeing them together. She dropped her gaze and focused on piping the frosting evenly. "How was your visit at Diamondback?"

"Good," he answered. "I got a good look at how they're running things over there. Those guys are smart."

"You're not moving into beef, are you?"

He shook his head. "No. And I don't want to build an operation that huge, either. But I have been thinking about trying some new stuff. Raising some sheep, maybe. Or some free-range chickens. The market's growing for both. Realistically I probably won't be able to buy up more quota for a bigger dairy herd. Anyway, right now it's just talk. I've got to do a lot more research and get things much more settled here before I look at expanding into something new."

She put down her decorating bag. "But you're excited about it, I can tell."

He grinned. Nell had a hold of one of his fingers and was shaking it up and down. "I *am* excited. I loved working on the farm in the summers when I was a kid. Never thought it'd be my livelihood, but I have no regrets about buying this place."

He belonged here. It wasn't like he could up and find another job in his field to be closer to his kid, was it?

Avery swallowed and reached for the tray of hats. "Sometimes you just never know what life has in store for you, do you?"

He laughed. "Your being here is a prime example of that." He leaned closer. "Are those *hats*?"

"Do you like them?" She put one in the palm of her hand. "I had to hand-shape them from the fondant. I think they turned out pretty well."

"That's amazing! Perfect for the rodeo, too." He nodded at the cakes. "Chocolate?"

"Sort of. Here. There's a spare. Try it."

She handed him a cake that was frosted but without the cowboy hat. Holding Nell tightly, he managed to peel off the cupcake paper and took a huge bite.

He chewed, swallowed and his eyebrows went up. "Whooo!"

"Chocolate and chili. I figured a rodeo would need a little kick."

"It shouldn't work, but it does."

"The cinnamon helps." She grinned. "They're really okay?"

He nodded. "Delicious. With a little added surprise."

"Good," she said, plucking a hat from the tray and placing it on the buttercream at a jaunty angle.

"Is there anything I can do to help?"

She was surprised at his offer but took him up on it because she knew that in a few days not only would he not be able to see Nell but Avery wouldn't be able to see him, either. And while she would never come right out and say so, she was going to miss him.

"There's a stack of bakery boxes over there. They need to be popped together. Other than that, I think everything's under control."

"I can do that."

He sat at the table and balanced Nell on his knee while taking the white cardboard boxes and tucking in the side tabs. In no time at all they were ready to go.

"What time do you have to have them at the grounds?" he asked. "If it's not too early, I can take you."

"Not until one. The chili cook-off starts then with the judging around four."

"Perfect. Gives me time to do what I need to here before watching the events."

"You mean you're coming?" Her mouth dropped open. "To the rodeo?" She didn't add the words "in public" and "with us" to the question, though she thought it. The man was so private, so conscious of minding his own business, that the idea of him not only taking them there but staying for the afternoon was surprising.

"Sam and Ty convinced me, saying it's not to be missed. Did you know Ty used to be a bull rider?"

Avery blinked. "Really?"

"A pretty good one, too. He retired when he came back to the ranch and married Clara. Besides, you're going to be busy, so we can trade-off looking after Nell."

She nearly bobbled the fondant hat in her hand.

"That sounds great," she answered. "I'll make sure I pack what she needs for the afternoon."

"I've got to head out to the barn. She's okay here now, right?"

"Of course." Avery felt badly that Nell was going to be put in her carrier yet again—even though she had the activity bar that snapped on. Back home she had a saucer that Nell could sit in and be surrounded by brightly colored and textured toys. If she'd known how long they were going to be here...

But nothing about this trip had gone to plan. And in some ways she was very glad.

He buckled the T-straps easily. "Bye, pumpkin." He pressed a kiss to Nell's forehead and then was gone.

Avery melted.

All day she'd gone back and forth about what to do, finally telling herself it was crazy to think about uprooting her life. Reminding herself that all along she'd had a plan to make it work. Callum had a home office. They could keep in touch by video in between visits, and she could send pictures.

But there'd be no kisses, no playtimes, no rocks before bed or tucking her under the covers for Callum.

More confused than ever, Avery went to work filling the boxes with the cakes. And when Nell started to cry, Avery found herself close to tears as well.

CHAPTER TEN

THE DAY COULDN'T possibly have dawned more perfect. The August sky was a clear, unmarred blue, the temperature forecast to be hot but not scorching, and a fresh breeze made the heads of the daisies bob merrily. When they arrived at the fairgrounds, Callum put Nell in her stroller while Avery took a stack of cupcake boxes and headed for the shaded tent set up for Butterfly House's event. Clara followed her back to the truck and helped bring along the last of the treats, grinning from ear to ear.

"What's got you so happy this afternoon?" Avery asked.

"Oh, this and that. It's a beautiful day and there's going to be lots of fun. Are you and Callum staying for the dance and fireworks later?"

There was a dance? And fireworks? Avery swallowed and took a moment to absorb the sound of her and Callum being paired up in conversation. It gave her a funny, tingling sensation that she knew came from fantasy and not reality. "Probably not. Callum will want to get back to do the milking."

"That's too bad. Well, maybe he'll change his mind. Though to be honest, even seeing him here today with Nell is quite something, isn't it? He's always been so reserved."

"I'm as surprised as you are," Avery admitted. "But he

said that I'd have trouble trying to manage Nell and man the cupcake station, so he'd come along."

Avery caught sight of the two of them heading toward the stands; the afternoon's events were going to begin soon. Her heart seemed to go all mushy as she watched his tall, lean figure pushing the stroller and carrying a pink-and-white diaper bag.

"Hey, are we going to set these out or what?" Clara's voice jolted her out of her stupor and she reluctantly pulled her gaze away from Callum.

"Oh, sorry."

"Can't blame you for being a bit distracted. Callum's a good-looking man. Especially since he cut his hair. I wonder why he did that?"

Avery focused on the bakery boxes rather than looking at Clara. "Nell was pulling on it, and Callum isn't quite the ponytail type."

Clara laughed. "Are you sure it didn't have something to do with you?"

It was torture, trying to keep her voice even and her body language nonchalant. She couldn't deny that his appearance set her pulse racing, especially since the new haircut seemed to bring out the intensity in his eyes. "I'm sure. It's all about Nell."

Angela came over then, with baby Ryan tucked in a Snugli carrier. His tiny head poked out, covered with a blue sun hat. "Hey, how did you two manage to end up kidless today?"

Clara shrugged. "Molly's got Susanna and is bringing her later. And Callum has Nell with him."

Angela's gaze flew to Avery's face. "How did you convince Callum to come? And to watch the baby? There's no way Sam or Ty would do it. They insist that they need to be around the livestock, blah blah."

Avery laughed. "He offered."

"Dairy farmer," Clara supplied.

Angela and Clara laughed and Avery knew they were joking but the offhand comment did make her a bit defensive. "He says he's talked to Ty and Sam and he's thinking about expanding and raising some sheep and maybe chickens. He says there's a growing market for grass-fed and free-range meat."

Clara's eyes softened. "We didn't mean anything against Callum," she apologized. "You've got to understand, though, that raising beef and rodeo…it's serious business around here. Especially for Ty. He only retired from bull riding a few years ago. Thank goodness. I like him safe and sound and in the stands."

Angela nodded. "Sam thinks Callum's a pretty smart guy, from what I gather. He just takes a while to warm up to people. I heard he was in the military before buying the farm. Sometimes transitioning can be difficult, you know?"

Angela had her social worker hat on but what she said made sense. What if part of Callum's problem wasn't Crystal or Jane at all, but something from his former life? Something he hadn't told her? She'd had the sense for some time that there was more bubbling beneath the surface of Callum Shepard.

More people arrived and Angela excused herself to help organize spots and make sure everyone had a power bar to plug in their Crock-Pot of chili. Clara helped Avery arrange the cupcakes on a couple of pretty stands that Avery had brought along.

"These hats are adorable! You didn't make these, did you?"

Pleased for the change of topic, Avery smiled and nodded. "Yes, I shaped them all by hand."

"All of them?"

Avery grinned. "Actually that's one of my favorite parts." She told Clara about the graduation order and the mortarboards complete with gold flake tassels. "And I came up with a special recipe today. I figured a rodeo cupcake needed some kick. Do you want to try one?"

Clara nodded. "Absolutely." She peeled off the paper and took a bite. Her blue eyes widened and met Avery's. "Whew! I wasn't expecting that!"

"Good, though, right?"

"What is that, chili?"

"Mostly cayenne."

"It really complements the chocolate. These are delicious! And so much better than what's at the bakery here. Don't get me wrong, they do an okay job, but there's not much invention if you know what I mean. You're going to do a brisk business today, you wait and see."

She was right. As the chili stand opened, the lineups began for a taste of the various recipes. The air around them was rich with the scent of tangy tomato and spice and there was a noticeable clink of coins as people paid a dollar for the chance to sample each kind. For another dollar they got a cupcake ticket, and more often than not people went back to pay fifty cents for a bottle of water that had been donated by a local supermarket.

Avery collected tickets and handed out cupcakes, getting several comments on the appearance of the treats. But best of all were the snippets of conversation she heard as they took their first bites.

This was the one reason why she hesitated making a move. She was so good at this, and the opportunity to run her own location was oh-so-tempting. It would also mean a more secure future for her and Nell, wouldn't it? She had that to consider, too. The Icing on Top was established and successful. In Cadence Creek she'd have to start building from scratch—and with a limited market.

The grandstand announcer's voice was calling events and her supply of cupcakes was dwindling when Callum showed up at the tent, pushing an empty stroller and Nell in his arms, her head nestled against his shoulder as she slept.

"She was fussy so I gave her the bottle you packed, and then she fell asleep. I thought I should get her out of the sun, though. It's pretty hot in the stands." He wiped his brow with his free hand. "Not much better in here."

"Come in behind the table. There's a fan behind me that's moving the air a bit. The judging is about to begin, and I'm starting to run out of cupcakes anyway. I only have maybe a dozen left."

"I heard a few people talking about them."

"Really?"

He nodded. "Said they wished there was somewhere to get things like that around here."

Avery smiled but her mind was turning. Clara had commented about the local bakery and she'd had a few people ask if she were new in town and if she could do a wedding shower and birthday party. Of course she'd had to turn them down, but she'd been flattered just the same.

It meant there was an opportunity here, but it also meant she'd have to do a lot of thinking. Making the treats for today was one thing, but this wasn't the type of venture she could run out of a regular home kitchen. And anything else meant a lot of start-up money.

"I'm glad they're a hit," she said as she accepted another ticket and handed over a cupcake and napkin with a smile.

Callum hung around for a few minutes as the judging took place, the ribbons were handed out and the last cupcake left the box. She tidied up her area as Angela counted the take for the afternoon. Molly Diamond showed up with a curly-topped Susanna itching to see her mother.

"Nice to meet you, Avery," Molly said, smiling. "I brought Susanna over to watch the last of the events. Have you had a chance to see anything yet?"

"I've been manning the cupcake station," she confessed.

"Why don't you come with us? Callum, I think Sam and Ty were looking for you, down on the south side of the arena."

"You're okay to take her?" Callum asked.

"Of course. Thanks for keeping her all afternoon. Go, have fun with the boys."

He grinned, that rare, lightning-fast smile that stole her breath. "I won't be long. I have to get back to do the milking."

"That's fine. See you in a bit."

She followed the Diamond women to the stands, relieved when they chose a section that wasn't in the direct sunlight. Ryan was spooling up after his nap and Angela fed him, and Clara kept the precocious Susanna occupied with a container of Goldfish crackers and a sippy cup. The saddle bronc event was just finishing up and the deep voice of the announcer told the crowd that during a short intermission before the final event—bull riding—there would be a wild cow milking contest.

Angela laughed. "This is one of my favorite parts—next to the mutton busting."

"Mutton busting?" Avery looked over, intrigued.

Molly grinned. "Kids riding sheep. Cute as all get-out. Ty loved it. I think we should have realized right then that rodeo was in his blood."

The first team came out and Avery found herself grinning as they roped the animal and one brave member had

to squeeze the milk into a glass bottle. The time was re-
corded, the arena cleared and the next team poised to go.

"And now we have the Diamond team set to go, and
hoo-eee, they brought themselves in a ringer this year.
Now we all know that this is beef country, but this gent
might just come in handy today. This afternoon's milker
for the Diamond team is Callum Shepard. Sorry, Callum,
couldn't find you a Holstein. This old girl'll have to do."

Avery's hand flew to her mouth. "This is what Ty and
Sam wanted him for?"

Clara burst out laughing. "Yep. I think Ty's words were
'it's about time he got welcomed to the community.'"

"Did you both know about this?"

Angela grinned, patting Ryan on the back. "Of course."

Butterflies turned over in Avery's stomach. Goodness,
Callum had no experience with rodeo! And though this
was a fun event, it still was dangerous. She'd seen the last
animal fight against the ropes, hooves going in every direction. She bit down on her lip as the bell rang and the
cow—and roping team—came rushing into the ring.

Roping the animal went quite smoothly when all was
said and done, and Callum moved in with the bottle and
hands at the ready. But the cow jolted, kicking over the
bottle and he had to put it upright again. Finally he got
some milk in the bottom and ran it to the judge. Ty and
Sam and one of their hired hands took off their cowboy
hats and raised their arms, swinging them around, while
Callum merely lifted a hand in a wave to the crowd.

"Looks to me like that feller needs a decent hat," the
announcer suggested. "Anyone got one handy?"

And out came a hat—a brown cowboy hat carried by
one of the rodeo princesses, dressed in full Western gear
with her satin sash across her chest. Cheers and whistles
went up from the crowd as he accepted it and plopped it

on his head—and more whistles as the girl stood on tip-toe and kissed his cheek. She left the arena and Callum took off the hat, acknowledged the crowd and then placed it back on his head again before leaving the arena, Ty and Sam giving him claps on the back.

They didn't win, and fifteen minutes later, just after the final event of the afternoon got started, he showed up in the stands. He lifted a hand to people who smiled and gave him a welcoming nod, and his face was a telltale shade of crimson beneath his tan when he finally got to Avery's side and sat down.

"Nice hat," she commented dryly.

"Those guys," he said, but there was humor in his voice. "I didn't know they were planning that until it was too late."

Avery looked over at him and grinned. "Admit it. You had fun."

"I did." His lips twitched.

"When did you last have fun, Callum?"

A shadow passed over his face. "A long time ago."

Once again she'd wondered if there was more to Angela's earlier comment. But now was not the time or place to ask, so she settled Nell on her lap and simply smiled. "Well, it was long overdue, then."

The tension in his shoulders relaxed and he looked at Nell. "The sun hasn't seemed to bother her."

"It's cooling off a bit now, especially in the shade. I should probably change her somewhere."

"She's a real trooper, Avery. A really good baby. If I haven't said it before, you've done a great job with her."

He kept his gaze trained on the bull bucking its way across the sandy floor of the arena, but Avery didn't doubt that he meant every word. The compliment meant so much, and she wished things were different. Wished—for the first time ever—that he'd chosen to take that walk with her through the garden in Niagara Falls instead of following the allure of something faster and brighter. Then instantly felt guilty.

"You've stepped up way more than I ever expected," Avery replied quietly, not wanting to be overheard by the Diamonds but feeling it needed to be said. "Whatever happens, Callum, she's going to be okay because we both want what's best for her. I'm glad of that. Glad she's going to know her dad even if she'll never know her mom."

"She has you," he answered. "She's a lucky kid." The conversation was getting a little heavy and he broke the tension with a smile. He patted his belly. "And as long as she's with you she'll never go hungry. You've spoiled me. It's not going to be easy to go back to my cooking after you're gone."

Gone. She couldn't forget that part. Couldn't afford to forget it for a moment. Not once had Callum ever hinted that she should stay. Those thoughts were hers and hers alone, brought on by her feelings for him and the way she'd grown to love the town in such a short time. He'd simply accepted that she was going back to Ontario.

Maybe he wouldn't even welcome such a move. He'd be close to his daughter, but that didn't mean he really wanted to be close to her, did it? A few kisses did not a future make.

"I've got to get back to do the chores," he said, checking his watch, indicating that the topic was closed. "It's getting on."

Leaving then, without staying for the evening festivities. Avery was a little disappointed. "Just let me get her things together, and I need to stop by the tent for the cupcake stands I bought." She didn't know what she was going to do with them now; it wasn't like she could take them with her on the plane. Maybe she'd donate them to Butterfly House for future events.

Clara looked up as they prepared to leave. "Are you going already? But you only got to see a little bit this afternoon. It'd be a shame for you to miss out on more of your first rodeo."

Avery was torn. She did want to stay but she didn't want to inconvenience Callum, especially since he'd already been so great. "It's okay," she replied. "It's been a great afternoon."

Callum shifted his feet. "Do you want to stay for a while? I can go milk and come back."

Clara nudged Avery's arm. "See? We're all staying, and you can hang with us until Callum gets back. We're going to set up shop in the Butterfly House tent over the supper hour so we can relax and have something to eat."

"Are you sure?" Avery looked up at Callum. It was so hard to read his eyes sometimes, and she didn't want him to feel pressured.

"I'm sure. I'll come back, and if it seems too much for Nell, we can take her back home again."

"All right. As long as it's okay with the Diamonds."

There was an awkward moment where Callum paused before saying goodbye, where it felt like a kiss would be a natural move and yet unnatural at the same time. In the end he touched a finger to Nell's downy head and walked off, leaving Avery with a tempting rear view.

It wasn't until they were walking back to the tent after the bull riding that Clara nudged her elbow again. "You have feelings for him, don't you?"

"Who?" Avery asked, though she knew very well who Clara meant.

Clara laughed. "It's written all over your face when you

look at him. You don't want to think of him that way, but you can't help it."

Avery's cheeks went hot. "You can see all that? Do you think he can?"

Clara shook her head. "I have no idea. But I know that look. I wore it often enough when I was fighting my feelings for Ty." She looked up ahead at her husband, her eyes luminous. "He's the best thing that ever happened to me."

"It's awkward with Callum. Nell is my niece. Plus, I live so far away, you know?"

"So move here. Unless there's someone back home…"

Clara let the thought hang. Avery considered lying so there'd be an end to the topic, but the truth was she liked Clara, and Angela, and all the Diamonds she'd met so far. Not only that, but other than her boss, Avery hadn't had anyone to confide in since Crystal's death. She blinked away a sudden stinging in her eyes. So many times something would happen with Nell and Avery would simply want to share it with Crystal—fully aware that it should have been Crystal experiencing those moments all along.

"No, there's no one back home."

"Then why not?"

"Because it's already weird between us. And it would be foolish to make such a big decision based on feelings I don't even know are real. Or if they'd ever be returned. It's not sensible, Clara."

Clara smiled. They reached the tent. Molly had spread out a blanket and Clara deposited Susanna in the middle and offered her several toys from a bag to keep her busy. "You sound like me, you know. I was pregnant with Susanna when Ty proposed. I didn't want to make that kind of decision without love. Sometimes you have to have a little faith that it'll all work out."

Avery sat down in a lawn chair and sighed. "I've never been too strong on the faith thing."

Clara sat down beside her and put a hand on her tummy. "I get it. But you know there are other good reasons. Nell would be closer to her daddy. After today's success, there's definitely room for you to do business here in town. And besides…" Clara smiled at her and put a hand on her arm. "You already have friends here, and a support system. With or without Callum. Cadence Creek is wonderful that way, Avery."

"I won't say the thought hasn't crossed my mind," Avery admitted. "I've grown to like this place a lot in the few weeks I've been here. It's just such a huge step. Not something I can do on a whim."

"Well, no one's saying you need to decide now. But just be open to the idea. I don't think Callum is as oblivious as you think he is. I've seen how he looks at you, too."

"Yeah, and if we screw it up, it's Nell who will pay for it."

Clara didn't have a reply to that, but she'd planted the seed in Avery's head. As the women looked after the kids and rested their feet, Ty and Sam went in search of supper. Nell was freshly changed and in pink-footed sleepers when the men returned with a stack of foil-wrapped sandwiches and a bag of soft drinks.

As Avery ate her meal she watched the Diamonds interact with each other. There was good-natured teasing, a helping hand, an easiness they all shared that Avery envied. It had never been that way in her house. It was the kind of family Nell deserved, big and boisterous and generous, and for today Avery was a part of it. But only a small part, because she knew it wasn't real. This wasn't her family—they were only on loan.

When the chuck wagon races were about to begin, Avery was feeling slightly overwhelmed by all her feelings and the well-intentioned advice she'd received, and she declined the invitation to join the Diamonds to the stands. "Nell's nearly asleep," she said quietly. "I think I'll wait for Callum here."

Inside the tent it was quiet and the background noises of people talking, country music, and the occasional announcement on the loudspeaker all served to relax her more. Nell, fed and changed and tired from all the fresh air, figured out it was close to her bedtime and her lids drooped. Avery retrieved a light blanket from the diaper bag and put it over both of them. She swallowed, imagined hopping on a plane in a few short days and her heart hurt.

What if she did decide to move here anyway? Clara was right. There were good reasons to consider it even if she left her feelings for Callum out of the equation.

What would it be like to live in a town like this, small and welcoming? What if she could open her own business, be her own boss? She imagined having a little storefront on Main Street with a striped awning, glass counters inside lined with cakes, tortes, cupcakes, all her own original creations. And maybe Nell would come in, cheeks rosy and hair mussed from an afternoon of playing with Susanna and Ryan and other neighborhood children.

She swallowed against the lump in her throat. It sounded perfect. The childhood she'd always wanted rather than a selection of apartments in various cities, more concrete than grass. The few parks near her apartment had to be monitored for drug dealings and other dangerous items left lying around like sharps and used condoms. It was hardly idyllic.

If only…

* * *

A warm hand squeezed her knee. "Avery."

"Hmm?" she asked, her eyes still closed.

"It's Callum."

"Callum," she said, and raised her hand, touching his face with her fingertips. She let out a sigh. She'd been dreaming, half in and half out of sleep, thinking about Callum and his eyes and his long legs and the way he looked when he smiled.

It was so warm and cozy. She dug under Nell's blanket more, willing the dream to come back.

"Avery," he said again, softly.

And then she knew she wasn't dreaming and her eyes opened. Callum was kneeling by her chair, freshly showered, looking up at her with his beautiful eyes.

And she knew that despite all the justifications, she couldn't move to Cadence Creek. Not and be this near to Callum. It wouldn't do any of them any good if she fell in love with him—and she was smart enough to know that she was already more than halfway there.

CHAPTER ELEVEN

CALLUM'S HEART SEEMED to pound clear up in his throat as he knelt before Avery. Coming here today had been bittersweet. He had already fallen for Nell, and now he felt himself making that slow, sickening slide with Avery. It scared the hell out of him. She was so…perfect. Beautiful without feeling the need to flaunt it. A perfect mother, a nurturing heart and a hard worker.

Which he might have been able to ignore except he'd already kissed her once and he knew what she could do to his heart rate. Dammit, she made him want things that he'd vowed never to want again.

And the stupid thing was he wanted to trust her. His gut told him he could.

Then again, he'd been down that road before, too, hadn't he?

"Avery," he said again, squeezing her knee. "It's Callum."

"Callum," she murmured sleepily, and she raised her hand and touched his face. He closed his eyes for a moment, enjoying the simple touch.

An idea had taken hold today and he was still playing around with it in his mind. She fit in here. She'd made friends and Callum had actually enjoyed getting out to the community event—even when it had meant revealing that Nell was his kid. The past few weeks he'd had a lot of time to think about the last year and the decisions he'd made. He knew one thing for sure. He hadn't been raised to turn his back on his responsibilities. And Nell was far more than that. She was *family*.

The problem was Avery and figuring out how she fit into everything. At times she looked at him like the sun rose and set in him. In others she was polite and utterly platonic. If he asked her to stay, he wondered if she'd get the wrong idea.

Or if he even knew what the *right* idea was.

"Callum," she said, stronger now, as she came awake.

He smiled. "Hey, sleepyhead. Sorry I took so long coming back. You two okay?"

She nodded. "I stayed back from the chuck wagon races. Nell was nearly asleep, and I was comfortable."

"We can go if you like. We don't need to stay."

"It's up to you." She smiled softly. "Everything okay at home?"

His heart gave a little kick as she called it *home*. It had been more of a home in the last week than it had ever been before. It had nothing to do with the fact that she'd managed to keep it tidy while he worked or that he'd been able to eat more than sandwiches and bacon and eggs. It was that she'd brought life to it—both her and Nell together. Before they came, it had been a place to eat and sleep. Now he looked forward to going back to the house at the end of the day.

The Diamonds approached and he stood up, sliding his hand off her knee. "Everything's fine."

The Diamonds greeted Callum and everyone chatted for a few minutes until Molly spoke up. "Well, I think I'll head out."

"You're not staying for the dance?" Sam asked.

"No, I'll leave that to you young people," she answered.

Clara looked up at Ty. "I think I'd like to go home, too, Ty. I'm really tired."

Ty looked down at Clara with concern. "Everything okay?"

She smiled. "Yes. It's just been a long day."

Molly's eyes narrowed. "It's eight o'clock. Only reason I can think of for someone your age to be tuckered out is that she might have an announcement to make."

Clara's cheeks pinkened. "I might. We might." She grinned, put her hand on her tummy. "Due in March."

As the group erupted in congratulations, Callum felt a bittersweet pang remembering the night Jane had told him about the baby. The excitement, the fear, the gravity of it. A future of possibilities. He'd shut that part of himself away for a long time but it broke loose now, making him momentarily jealous of Ty and Clara. He knew how Ty was feeling right now—about ten feet tall. It was written all over his face. Callum stole a look down at Avery. She was smiling and she stepped forward to offer her congratulations, but there was a wobble in the way she held her lips, too, that made him believe the news made her a little bit sad. Was she thinking about Crystal? Did she have bad memories to blend with the good, like he did?

Clara squeezed Avery's hand. "Why don't you send Nell home with us? That way you and Callum can enjoy the dance without worrying about the baby. We have lots of everything. You, too, Angela. When was the last time you and Sam had an evening alone since Ryan was born?"

Molly nodded. "I never mind having grandchildren around. You can always pick her up later, Callum, or just come by in the morning."

It startled him that after such a brief association, he was made to feel like a part of the family. And it made him miss his own family, especially his brother and sister. This is how things should be between siblings.

His parents were nearing retirement and had looked forward to grandkids. They'd made no secret of it, until the wedding had been called off. Now it was a topic that was never discussed. Hell, he hadn't even phoned them to tell them this latest news. Maybe because he wasn't sure if they'd be happy or disappointed in him.

Avery's voice interrupted his thoughts. "I don't know," she said, her voice hesitant. She looked back at Callum. "What do you think?"

She was asking him? It felt, oddly enough, like a compliment that she would defer to him when she usually—and quite rightly—took the lead when it came to parenting. "It's up to you," he replied, but he was thinking that the idea of a few hours alone with Avery could be a very good—and bad—thing. Up to this point it had all been about spending time with Nell. Now it was spending time together.

"You're sure you don't mind?" Avery asked Clara. "You said you were tired. I don't want to impose."

"I'm not going to fall over." Clara laughed. "I'm just not up to dancing. Believe me, it's no trouble, as long as you have your car seat."

Avery looked up at Callum. "What do you say?"

He trusted the Diamonds completely, but Avery's eyes held a shadow of worry. "If you'd like to stay, I know Nell will be perfectly fine with them."

"It would be fun," she relented, a wistful note in her voice. "I just haven't left her before."

"You can always leave Clara your cell number and she can call if she needs anything."

Avery nodded and turned back to Clara. "Okay," she said, smiling. "And thank you. I haven't had a night out since she was born. We'll get her car seat and everything you should need is in the diaper bag."

Molly touched Avery's arm. "It's always hard leaving them for the first time. You enjoy yourself and I don't want to see you until morning. Might as well let her sleep rather than get her up again later."

"I don't know what to say," Avery replied.

Callum stepped up. "We really appreciate it. I'll go get her seat and meet you at Ty's truck, Clara."

In a handful of minutes they had all the kids buckled in and diaper bags sorted and Callum watched as Ty and Clara drove off with his daughter. He swallowed around a lump in his throat. Avery stood by his shoulder and he reached down and took her hand. "A few weeks ago I didn't know she even existed and now I feel so strange watching her drive away." He squeezed her fingers and decided to be brutally honest. "I can't imagine what it's going to feel like watching her fly away in a few days."

Music started up in the community hall and the sounds echoed, slightly distorted, to where they stood in the parking lot. Avery squeezed back. "I know. Let's not think about it now, okay? Let's check out the dance with Angela and Sam and kick up our heels. It's the perfect ending to a fun day and I might not get the chance to have the authentic experience again."

They joined the others at the hall where the country music was thumping enthusiastically and already couples were swinging around the floor in a two-step. He bought them each a soft drink and they stood on the fringes, just watching the stomping, circling crowd for a while.

It had been a long time since he'd felt a part of anything. It used to be the army, until his personal life fell apart and then he'd screwed that up big-time, leaving before he could be forced out. For months it had seemed like there was nowhere he belonged. But today...today had changed all that. Today he became a member of the town—right down to the boots and Smithbilt hat. He had friends again. None of that would have happened without the advent of Avery in his life. Without her—without Nell—he'd still be sitting at home, licking his wounds.

After a fast set, the music slowed. "Care to?" he asked, holding out his hand.

She bit down on her lip, the way she did when she was nervous, he realized. It gave him confidence. It wasn't just him. She was feeling it, too. He had to tread carefully but there was something there, and if they didn't address it tonight, there wouldn't be another chance, would there?

"Did you come to watch or did you come to dance?" he asked.

She put her hand in his and he led her out on the floor. Stopped and put his hand on her waist, then turned the other and captured her fingers in his. Her left hand skimmed his ribs and he inhaled sharply.

And then, because he couldn't help himself, he slid his hand to the small of her back and drew her closer as they started to move.

Avery's whole body was on high alert, especially with the warmth of Callum's wide hand seeping through the waistband of her jeans. In boots and his new hat, he was more tall and imposing than ever, but no longer frightening— at least not in the way she'd initially imagined. There was a gentleness to him she'd missed the first few days she'd been in Cadence Creek. He'd relaxed since then, been more like the man she remembered meeting all those months ago, except maybe more cautious and guarded.

Now, without Nell between them, this felt very much like a date. Maybe it was wishful thinking, but when Clara had offered to take the baby for the night, there'd been a light in Callum's eyes. As they moved on the dance floor, she realized quite suddenly that they were going to be completely alone at the house tonight.

As if he could read her thoughts, he pulled her closer until their bodies brushed and the song shifted into another slow one, this time a waltz. He lowered his head and caught her gaze. "Can you waltz?" he asked.

She nodded even as the electricity between them seemed to spike. His hand pressed even more firmly on her back and he caught the beat, moving smoothly into the rocking three-count rhythm.

She was waltzing with Callum Shepard at a rodeo dance. It seemed utterly surreal and strangely perfect.

When the song was over, he paused for a moment before letting her go. "Thanks," he murmured, and she nodded, backing out of his embrace and hoping her cheeks weren't blazing as hotly as she thought they were.

They met up with Sam and Angela on the sidelines and got another cool drink as the room heated up. When the next two-step came on, Sam held out his hand for Avery. "Do you know how?"

She shook her head. "Not at all."

He waggled his hand. "Then it's time you learned. Come on."

She looked up at Callum, who was grinning at her smugly. "Go ahead."

"You're not off the hook," Angela said, grabbing Callum's hand. "You have to learn, too."

Avery laughed as he pulled back. "Uh, I don't think so," he protested.

"Come on. If she has to, you have to."

Avery giggled as Sam instructed her in the counting of

the steps. "Okay," he said, "once you get the rhythm down, I'll show you how to do turns."

It took a minute or two, and every now and again she'd slip in her count and add an extra step, but before long they were moving smoothly. She looked over and saw Callum leading Angela with a smile on his face. He moved his hand and Angela slid beneath his arm, executing a perfect turn. Avery was so caught up with watching that she tripped and Sam kept her upright with a strong hand.

"They're showing us up. What do you think, are you ready to go under?"

"I don't know…"

"Just let my hand guide you, and when you come back step on the one."

The first try she was a little off, but by the second she was good. And by the bridge of the song he'd maneuvered them closer to Angela and Callum and then deftly switched partners so she was in Callum's embrace again.

He grinned as they picked up the steps, somewhat less confident than they'd been with their previous partners but managing just the same. "Having fun?" he asked.

She nodded, amazed when he lifted his hand and guided her through a turn. "You've got natural rhythm, Callum."

His gray eyes caught hers and held and the room seemed suddenly overwarm.

The song ended and Avery deliberately put some space between her and Callum. She chatted to a few ladies about her cupcakes and watched as Callum talked to some local ranchers along with Sam. She was always aware of where he was, and when the band announced a break for the fireworks display, he found her with his eyes and raised his eyebrows, a silent question. Were they going to go outdoors with the others?

They met at the door to the hall and stepped outside

where it was surprisingly cool after the heat from the dancing.

"Where do you want to watch?"

She shrugged. "I don't know, anywhere, I suppose. We don't have anything to sit on."

"I can fix that. Wait here."

He jogged off to the parking lot and came back a minute later with a scratchy wool blanket. "I always keep it in the back for emergencies," he explained. "Not that this is an emergency, but it'll at least keep us off the dirt."

They placed it on the ground among the group that had gathered and Avery sat, crossing her legs and resting her elbows on her knees. It had been such a perfect day, and she realized with some surprise that she was going to miss the town, too. Callum lifted a hand to wave at someone and Avery understood that it was the sort of place where neighbors knew each other and helped each other. She'd never lived anywhere quite like it, hadn't even been sure such a place actually existed.

Callum sat beside her, stretched out his long legs and leaned back on his elbows. He'd removed his hat and placed it on the blanket beside him, and she noticed it had flattened a ring of hair around his head. She longed to reach out and ruffle the dark strands, but after that last dance and her unintentional innuendo, she kept her hands to herself.

The first burst exploded in the sky, and a chorus of "oohs" rippled through the crowd, punctuated by sounds of delight coming from the children. Once it got started, the rockets kept coming at a regular tempo, lighting up the night with colorful cascades after each pop. Avery looked over at Callum, surprised to see his jaw tense and a muscle there tick tightly as the sound exploded. He was staring straight ahead, not at the display above them. Avery's stomach knotted. He wasn't enjoying it for whatever reason.

Then a series of fireworks exploded straight up, one after another, long tails and flashes and Callum flinched after each sharp report.

Finally the display ended and the crowd clapped and cheered. Avery did, too, but only politely as Callum picked up his hat and settled it on his head.

As people dispersed, heading back to the hall, Callum turned his head to her. "You ready to go back in?"

She got the feeling that going back to the gaiety of the dance was the last thing Callum wanted, and it had already been a long day. "I think I've had my fill. Why don't we just go home?"

Was that relief she saw on his face? It was hard to tell, the way it was shadowed, but she didn't miss the quick nod. "That's fine, then. If you're tired."

She didn't dispute it and they folded up the blanket. Avery carried it in her arms as they made their way to the parking lot and Callum unlocked the truck. They were halfway home before Avery got up the courage to ask.

"The fireworks bothered you, didn't they?"

He stared out the windshield. "Of course not."

What had she expected? It would be unlike Callum to admit any weakness. Even explaining about Jane had been grudging at best, though it had at least paved the way toward a new status quo between them as coparents. This had nothing to do with Nell, or Jane, or anyone else other than Callum.

"I just thought…Angela said something today that got me thinking, that's all."

"About what?"

"You and I talked about Jane, but we never talked about what you did before. Your job. You're a really private man,

Callum. You were practically living like a hermit. Angela was saying that sometimes transitioning out of the forces can be difficult…"

"You told her about Jane?" Anger tinged his words.

"No, of course not. She just said that up until recently, you've been a bit of a loner. I wouldn't share something you told me in confidence."

He visibly relaxed, but only a bit. "Angela's a social worker," he said shortly. "I like her, don't get me wrong, but really, I'm fine."

"Then why were you hiding away on your farm when we showed up? The last few days…you've been much more the man I remember meeting at Pete and Elizabeth's wedding. Then during the fireworks, that scowl on your face." She frowned. "It reminded me of how you looked that first day I knocked on your door and you asked me what I wanted."

He turned onto the dirt road that led to his place. "Leave it alone, Avery. We had a nice day. Let's just leave it at that."

Rebuffed, she turned her head to stare out the window. There were no streetlights out here, nothing but the inky-blackness of the prairie meeting the gently rolling foothills. He'd left the light by the front door on, though, and once he'd parked she got out of the truck and headed straight for the door.

Which he'd locked.

She waited while he came up behind her and put the key in the lock. The door swung open and Avery put her purse on the floor.

"Well, good night, then," she said weakly, not having a clue what else to say. It had been going so well, with the dancing and the long looks and the way he'd held her hand when she'd decided to let go of Nell for the night. Now he was completely closed off to her.

She was nearly to the hall when his voice stopped her. "Avery, wait."

She stopped, but didn't turn around. She wished now she'd flicked on a light when she'd come in the door. Something to dispel the intimacy of the darkness around them.

"You're right. The fireworks probably weren't a good idea. I didn't know that I'd...well, you know."

She did turn then. He was standing close to the door, his hand still on the knob, like he was ready to make his escape at any moment. He couldn't even say it. She understood anyway. He hadn't realized he'd react as he had. "Why did you?"

He took off his hat and held it in his hands. "It's a long story."

"I gathered that. But Jane's deception was awful, and yet you managed to tell me about it. This, then, must be worse."

"It is." There was a long pause until he finally relented with a sigh. "You knew Pete."

"Of course. I was a bridesmaid at the wedding, remember?"

"And you knew we were deployed together. Including the tour where he didn't come home, not long after the wedding."

Elizabeth and Peter had moved to the new base, and Avery remembered hearing the news. Crystal had already discovered she was expecting a baby and didn't want anyone to put two and two together, so they'd sent flowers in lieu of traveling for the memorial. In the weeks following, the friendship with Elizabeth had drifted apart. "I knew you were part of the same regiment."

"Closer than that. We were in the same section. Like a squad, you know?"

She didn't know much about military configuration but she understood it meant they were in a small group together. "Were you hurt the day he was killed, Callum?"

She asked it gently; it was a difficult question to ask.

"Not a scratch. Not for me, the section screwup." His voice was harsh and self-mocking. "I didn't want to be there—in Afghanistan. I didn't want to be anywhere. I was bitter about Jane and angry at life and a jackass. The morning that patrol went out, I was sleeping it off. Not fit for duty." He huffed out a bitter laugh. "Hell, I wasn't fit for duty anyway, even when I was sober."

Avery took a step forward, finally understanding. He'd been punishing himself because of a huge case of survivor's guilt. "So you feel you failed them?"

"I should have been there. Hell, it should have been me, not them. The fireworks tonight…they sounded like…"

She tilted her head and studied him. Like what? Gunfire? Mortars? "But if you'd been there," she reasoned, "the only thing that would have happened is you would have died, too."

"Maybe I could have saved them."

"And maybe you all would have been lost."

"That doesn't do a damn thing for my conscience." He tossed his hat on a chair. "You want to know why it scares me to death to be a father? Because I mess things up for everyone in my life. Jane couldn't handle me being gone all the time and I ignored her when she asked when I was getting out. Being married to a soldier was too hard for her. She didn't like being left alone and she couldn't handle wondering when or even if I'd come back. I knew it and pretended it didn't matter. She found someone else who would be there for her 24/7. Pete and the others…no matter what you say, I know I should have been there for them. Instead I was a self-indulgent idiot, half drunk and angry at the world. Face it, Avery. I'm a selfish bastard."

"But if you'd been with them that day, Nell wouldn't have a father, either."

"Give me time. I'm sure I'll screw that up, too."

He paused, then sighed. "Look, Avery. I pretended to forget all of that these last few weeks. You waltzed in with your smile and your damn cakes and…and everything, and I played along. Tonight was just the reminder I needed. Nell is way better off with you, Avery. We both know it."

"So you're going to, what, go back to being a recluse? Hibernating in this house? Forget about your daughter? You know what, Callum? That makes me angry." She didn't worry about keeping her voice down now, there was no baby to disturb. No one but the two of them in the dark. She took another step, closing the distance between them bit by bit as her temper flared. "Maybe you should have been with them but you weren't. For some reason you were spared. And instead of being down on your knees and thankful and living the life that they can't, you've buried yourself right along with them. That's what makes you a coward, Callum Shepard. Not the mistake you made, but your refusal to overcome it. That's a choice."

"So now you're going to lecture me?" he asked incredulously. "About living, when you were content to live in your sister's shadow for years?"

The words hit their mark and she flinched, but she answered truthfully. "I did do that. It was easier. But not anymore. I can't. I have Nell now, and her future to think of."

"And you're going to hide behind her, too, aren't you? She needs you. It's the perfect excuse for you. It's the perfect way to avoid intimacy or allowing someone too close.

You think I don't see that? I'm not as clueless as you seem to believe."

She was getting really angry now. All the things they'd held back over the last two weeks were coming out and they weren't pretty. The night had started out so amazing and was disintegrating at a rapid pace, and the thought of leaving here in a few days was suddenly tearing her apart. Why did he have to be so stubborn? So blind to what was right in front of him?

"You think I can't let people close? That I'm afraid of intimacy?"

She took the last two steps, closing the remaining distance between them and did what she'd been longing to do ever since the first time they'd kissed on the sofa. She curled her hand around his neck, pressed her body to his and pulled his head down for a kiss.

His lips were firm and warm and opened slightly in surprise, but only for the breath of a second. Maybe she initiated the contact but he took control now, wrapping an arm around her and pulling her close to his body as the kiss raged out of control. He ripped his mouth from hers, took a breath and let out a curse. "It wasn't a damn dare, Avery."

"You said you didn't want me to hide. So here I am. Are you going to run now, Callum?"

She was inviting him to a game of sexual chicken and she knew it, but she was tired of thinking—of overthinking—every single decision.

His answer was to kiss her again, sending her pulse clamoring to every part of her body. Somewhere in the back of her head a voice murmured that sleeping with him would be a mistake. But the voice that craved him, the part of her that listened to the ticking clock counting down to the moment she would leave, overruled it.

"Avery," he whispered.

His voice was not angry. The way he said her name was a tone of absolute acceptance. A quiet confirmation that she'd maybe broken through the barriers of resentment, of guilt and of pain. It held the featherlight wonder of seeing her—really seeing her—for the first time, weighted down by the gravity of feelings and responsibilities. Hearing her name on his lips brought a longing for him that was alternately exhilarating and terrifying.

"I'm right here," she answered, her throat tight.

"Tomorrow…"

She pressed her finger to his lips. "I don't want to think about tomorrow. That's all I ever do. Worry and plan and think. For once, let's worry about tomorrow when we get there."

His hand slid down her bare arm, past her wrist and came to rest on her hip, his fingers reaching dangerously close to the back pocket of her jeans. He kissed her again, slower now, without the fast burn of anger and frustration. With beautiful, wordless intent. Maybe it was a mistake but she didn't intend to stop him. It was messy, it was complicated and it was risky. But in her heart Avery also knew it was right. And that now that she understood the *why* of Callum, it could only get better. She had to believe that.

So when he slid an arm beneath her knees and lifted her into his embrace, she held on. His boots sounded hollow on the hardwood in the hall as they bypassed her bedroom and continued on to his.

And once he stepped inside, he closed the door, shutting them away from the rest of the world.

CHAPTER TWELVE

SUNLIGHT STREAMED INTO the room as Avery woke. The other side of the bed was empty, just as it had been yesterday morning when she'd awakened with the memory of him still imprinted on her skin. Callum would be out doing the milking and chores right now, but the scent of him was still on the sheets. Avery took a few moments to close her eyes and curl up in the soft cotton. Soon Nell would be awake and the day would start. Her last full day in Cadence Creek. Her last day with Callum.

She opened her eyes and looked at the ceiling. They'd agreed to avoid the topic of her leaving for the past thirty-six hours. Not talking about it didn't mean she hadn't thought about it constantly, though. More than ever, Avery felt the urge to start over, make a new life here in Cadence Creek.

But Callum hadn't so much as breathed a word about her staying. And as much as the last two nights had been fantastic, she knew they had to talk about it sooner or later. If he wasn't going to ask, they had to at least talk about how to proceed in the weeks and months ahead. For Nell's sake.

It wasn't a conversation she was looking forward to having. It was full of potential emotional land mines. She wasn't sure how she could get through it without revealing too many of her feelings. And as fantastic as the last two nights had been, it had only posed a bigger problem for Avery. She wouldn't be going back to Ontario with her heart in one piece. She'd fallen for Callum completely—the whole Callum. Not the man he'd pretended to be in Niagara Falls, not even the man who had danced with her at the community hall. But the man who'd shown her what he considered the very worst side of himself when he spoke of how his life had fallen apart, the mistakes he'd made. And still he'd been gentle with her, and patient, and best of all, giving. She hadn't known he could be like that. Hadn't known *any* man could.

They were right for each other. Somehow she had to make him see it, too.

She had a quick shower before getting Nell out of bed, the tot rubbing her fists in her eyes as she came awake. By the time Nell had had her breakfast bottle and Avery had started mixing eggs in a bowl, Callum was on his way in from the barn. Nerves bubbled around in Avery's stomach as he came in, gave Nell a kiss and then stopped by the stove where she was pouring the eggs in a pan for scrambling. He gave her a light kiss, too, sending her pulse racing.

"Morning," he said.

"Good morning." She tried a smile. "You hungry?"

"Starving." He rubbed his tummy and she turned to find him watching her with a twinkle in his eye.

She wanted to see that twinkle every morning. "Put some bread in the toaster, then, while I stir these."

"Yes, ma'am."

They worked around the kitchen for a while as Avery tried to find the right way to broach the subject. Nothing she came up with sounded right in her head.

"So what are your plans for today?" he asked, taking jam out of the fridge and putting it on the table.

She swallowed against the lump of nervousness in her throat. The smell of the eggs made her slightly nauseated as her appetite deserted her. "Well, probably packing our things. Our flight is scheduled for midmorning tomorrow."

"Right."

The toast popped, the noise abnormally loud in the quiet kitchen.

The eggs were done, so Avery made a show of putting them on plates, a much smaller portion on her own since she really wasn't feeling that hungry. They sat at the table, the silence stretching out until Avery thought it must pop like a rubber band if it got any tighter. If he would only just ask her to stay, give any indication that he wanted to be with her beyond today...

Callum put down his fork. "Avery, we need to talk about what comes next."

She let out a breath of relief. "I'm so glad to hear you say that. Yes, we do."

She lifted her eyes. It was so hard to tell what he was thinking, what he was feeling. He'd had a lot of practice at keeping himself guarded.

"You know I want to be a part of Nell's life," he said evenly. "But Nell isn't the only one to consider here. The last few days..."

The last few days they'd been together. Really together, in every way possible.

He lifted his chin. "Avery, I don't want to rush things, or put you on the spot. There are a lot of things to consider. You have your job and your apartment and a whole life back in Burlington. I just want you to keep an open mind about us. Nothing has to be decided now, right?" He smiled at her. "We can take it one day at a time. See how things go."

As far as a glowing declaration, it fell way short of the

mark. And yet Avery knew it was the cautious, sensible approach. It was the way she'd lived her whole life up to this point. Logically. Trusting her head and not her heart. Being sure she was on solid ground before taking another step. And it wasn't like he'd shut the door on them. He was just being careful.

The trouble was, she didn't want to live that way anymore.

"One day at a time," she echoed, without a lot of enthusiasm.

"I mean, we have to put Nell first, of course."

"Of course." He was totally right, so why did she feel so deflated? Then she wondered if perhaps she was being selfish and putting her feelings ahead of Nell's. She'd said from the first moment they'd felt this attraction that it would be a mistake. That if something went wrong Nell would be the one to pay. Had she forgotten that so easily?

She toyed with the corner of her piece of toast. No, she hadn't forgotten it. But she had gotten caught up in the idea of the *rightness* of this place that she'd constructed this white picket fence idea of what life here could be like.

Callum reached over and cupped her jaw in his hand. When she looked up at him, she couldn't help the tears that sprang to her eyes. She blinked, willing them away. The last thing she needed was to get overly emotional about the whole thing.

"Two weeks is such a short time," he said softly. "I'm not giving up. I just want us to take things slowly. Be sure. For all our sakes. Okay?"

She nodded, knew she should be happy. What had happened between them was nothing short of amazing. Instead there was a heavy weight settling in the pit of her stomach. Because she'd wanted him to say it. She'd wanted him to tell her to quit her job, set up a business here, move to Cadence Creek and live happily ever after. And if not happily ever after, at least be here while they figured out exactly what was between them.

"I'm glad I came," she said, picking up her fork and making a show of pushing around some eggs on her plate. "It's been a good trip. Surprising, but good."

He smiled. "*Surprising* doesn't begin to cover it."

They finished the meal and as Avery was clearing the dishes Callum looked out the window. "Mail's here already. I'm going to run out and bring it in. I'm expecting some information I emailed a company about last week."

When he came back, his brows were pulled together in a frown.

"What is it?" Avery asked.

"The test results. Can you believe it? I'd forgotten all about them."

He tossed the envelope on the table and instead tore open the seal to a bigger package.

"Aren't you going to open it?" she asked, surprised at his easy dismissal.

"Do I really have to?"

Avery understood and appreciated what he was saying, but the envelope sat there, waiting to be opened like unfinished business. She picked it up and ripped across the flap, taking out the paper inside.

The DNA results confirmed Callum as the father, and Avery closed her eyes and let out a relieved breath before handing the letter over to him.

Callum gave the paper a quick glance but his gaze quickly darted up to her face. She closed her eyes and let out a breath while something dark and familiar twisted at his heart. "You weren't sure?" he asked, his voice suddenly hoarse.

"What?" Her brow wrinkled as she stared up at him.

Callum stood very, very still. "I said," he stated in a low voice, "you weren't sure I was her father?"

"Don't be silly!" Avery straightened her shoulders. "Why would you say that?"

Oh, playing dumb was only making it worse. That blank, innocent expression cut through him like a knife. "Because of the look of relief on your face just now. The way you closed your eyes and let out your breath. Oh, my God. You actually had your doubts." All along she'd pretended to be so sure. She'd let him fall in love with his daughter knowing it could all be a farce. She'd let him fall in love with her...

No. She hadn't quite accomplished that, he told himself. He smacked the paper down on the table as his anger built. He should have known better than to fall for this again.

"Callum, no. I swear to you, up until the moment I saw the envelope, I didn't have a moment of doubt."

"And then?" he asked, his voice dangerously calm.

She looked down. "I don't know. I guess I needed to see it in black-and-white. I never knew anything about her feelings for Pete. What else hadn't she told me? What if Crystal hadn't told me the truth?"

He didn't believe her. He wanted to, and that was what hurt the worst. He'd ignored his gut instinct because he'd wanted to trust her so badly. Wanted to believe she wasn't another Jane. Oh, her intentions had been good, but in the end, he was the one left hurting.

"God, what a fool I've been!"

He spun away but she went after him, grabbing his arm. "A fool? You were the one who insisted on the stupid test in the first place, and then you acted like you didn't care about the results!"

"Because I trusted you." The words came through gritted teeth. "I looked at Nell and I was sure. But more than that, I trusted *you*. You were one hundred percent sure that Crystal had told the truth. Only you really weren't certain, were you? You just let me believe."

She swallowed. "I had no reason to doubt her."

"But you did anyway?" he pressed.

"No! Not at the time. Looking back now, I can see things I missed. Her decision not to tell you about being pregnant. What you said about her having a thing for Pete—we shared everything, don't you understand? But not that. God, no wonder she hadn't wanted to go to his memorial. She had her secrets from me, Callum, and you can't know how that hurts."

"Oh, really? Secrets from the sister who waltzed in here claiming to know everything there was to know about her?"

"Don't be nasty," she said firmly. "She was my sister. Even so, she was entitled to her secrets."

"And you thought this might be one of them. And still you came here, inserted yourself into my life, made me fall…"

He stopped abruptly, cleared his throat while Avery held her breath.

"Made me fall in love with Nell," he said, gentling his voice slightly. "Worse than that, you… We…"

"We made love. Can't you even say it, Callum?"

He couldn't. Not when his heart was this involved. She was the first one since Jane. She had no idea what she'd done. Yes, Nell was really his and nothing could change that. But the damage had been done. She'd been no better than Jane when it came down to it. At least Jane had finally come clean because she couldn't live with the deception.

"Why did we?" he asked. "I want to know, Avery. Was it all part of your master plan? What did you expect to gain from all this? I mean, you did make the first move. You must have had some idea of what you wanted. Did it even matter to you if I was Nell's real father or not?"

He regretted the words the instant he said them. She looked as if she'd been whipped and the hostility radiating out of him took away all the lovely moments they'd shared and twisted them into something cold and calculated. He mourned the loss of them.

"That's not it at all! Please, Callum, listen to me. It was a simple reaction, nothing more. I had a moment of doubt for a second or two when I looked at the letter, but it was wrong. I knew all along in my heart that Nell is yours! I wouldn't have come here otherwise. You have to believe me. I'm not capable of the things you're suggesting."

"How do I know that?" He felt the anger drain out of him, replaced with disappointment and despair. "All I know is the Avery I've seen in the last two weeks. You could have been out to fool me all along. Everything I told you, about Jane, about the guys..."

He sat down heavily. "I trusted you, Avery. And it makes me sick. You knew how badly Jane had hurt me. That alone should have ensured your honesty. You had plenty of opportunities."

"I'm going to say this one more time. I honestly did not have a moment of doubt until I saw that proof in black-and-white. What I can't control is whether or not you believe me."

He wanted to so badly it ached. Never had he felt so vulnerable. Not even when Jane had given him back his ring, and that was surprising. A lot had happened since then. He had been so happy when Jane had announced she was pregnant, and he'd mourned the loss of the life he'd almost had. The fact that Avery had known that, and would have put him through the same thing was enough to make him start shutting down the corners of his heart that he'd opened to her.

Unless, of course, she was telling the truth.

"I'm not her," Avery said quietly, squatting before him and putting her hand on his knee. "You think I came here with the intent to lure you into some trap, to what? Take care of me and Nell? I can take care of us both just fine, as I've been doing for several months now. Jane must have really done a number on you to make you doubt everything that comes out of my mouth. So here it is, Callum. You want to know the truth? Yes, for a space of a few seconds, I acknowledged somewhere in the back of my mind that there was a miniscule chance the results would be different. I'm human. I realize there were things I didn't know about my sister, okay? But it was a few seconds, that was all. Anything that has happened here in the last few weeks has been completely genuine on my part. Every single emotion—the bad and the good. Sleeping with you was no trap. Falling for you was not on the agenda. That doesn't mean it wasn't real."

He didn't answer for a few seconds as her words settled around them. He looked up in her eyes, so wide and blue and earnest. This woman had more power over him than anyone ever had before. He simply didn't have enough faith left inside him to take her at her word.

"I don't believe you."

She sighed, seemed to choose her words carefully. "You're scared to believe me. There's a difference. If I'm telling the truth you're going to have to deal with the feelings between us. And it means you have to trust me, which clearly you don't."

"I've trusted before, and look where that got me. I can't go through that again."

"Right. And because one person betrayed you everyone else in the world is bound to, too, right?"

He had to look away from her face, because she was silently crying now, tears slipping over her cheeks. He felt like crying himself. He'd finally allowed himself to hope again and one little moment had ripped it away.

"I understand betrayal. And I understood that you will never believe, never trust, in just words. I really don't have anything else to offer."

"Tell me," he asked. "How would you have spun it if the results had been different?"

She stepped back. He'd finally said the right thing to drive her away. Too bad he felt like crap about it.

"I get it," she said quietly. "Tomorrow we'll get on a plane for home, just as we planned."

"That's for the best," he said shortly. He had to get out of here. He made his escape to the only place he knew she wouldn't bother him—the barn. The screen door slapped in the frame behind him.

Avery stared at Callum crossing the yard. Thought about what he'd said and what he hadn't said. What he'd been through and how much he'd changed during her time there. And what she saw was a man who was scared to death of having his heart broken a second time. And this time with his own daughter in the mix, complicating things.

She loved him. She must, or the words he'd flung at her this morning wouldn't have hurt so much. She did love him, because as much as they hurt, she'd already forgiven him.

There was only one thing that Callum would understand. And it involved Avery taking the biggest risk of her life.

CHAPTER THIRTEEN

AVERY STOOD IN front of the storefront, gazing into the dusty windows. Tomorrow the real work would begin. The landlord was going to take out part of the wall separating the Cadence Creek Bakery from the other vacant space to make it one big store, with tables to sit at café-style. The bakery would continue to bake its fabulous breads and rolls, cookies and pies. The fancy cakes, though, that was going to be Avery's area of expertise. Joining forces had been the smartest thing to do—working with, rather than in competition against, the biggest baked-good supplier in town. It also meant lower overhead for Avery, as she had access to the bakery's equipment. It was a win-win—running her own shop without assuming the same level of risk.

The biggest risk was moving here in the first place. But whenever she started to get cold feet, she thought of Clara's words. Cadence Creek was a good town with good people, business opportunities and, as she'd reiterated during their phone calls, a built-in support system. Avery loved it with or without Callum, and she was excited about starting this new chapter in her life, and thrilled that Nell was going to grow up in the warm, small town.

The kicker was that Callum didn't know anything about her return. She'd sworn all the Diamonds to secrecy and she'd resisted the urge to tell him each time they spoke about Nell. The conversations were always polite but strained.

She'd been terribly afraid to tell him for fear he'd try to talk her out of it.

Nell kicked her legs in the stroller—the heavy-duty one this time—and with a laugh Avery wheeled her back to the car, which she'd parked on a side street in the shade. There was a different feel to Cadence Creek now in late September. The hanging baskets were still up on the lampposts but there was a laziness to the Indian summer heat, a fullness to it, that Avery enjoyed. She missed the bright colors of an Ontario autumn, but she found herself intrigued by the golden-hued prairie fall.

All along the drive out of town and south to Callum's place she admired the yellow poplar and birch leaves and the brown stubble of the harvested fields. A beat-up half ton truck she didn't recognize sat beside Callum's newer one.

Avery knocked on the door, doubting that she'd find him inside at this time of day. When the door swung open she caught her breath at the sight of him.

Callum wasn't dressed for work. He was in khaki pants and a dress shirt with his hair freshly cut and perfectly in place. Avery thought he'd never looked more wonderful.

"Avery! What in the world are you doing here?" he asked, coming forward with a wide smile and eyes only for Nell. "Oh, my gosh. She's grown so much and it's barely been more than a month."

He reached out and grabbed Nell, propping her up on his elbow as he gave her a kiss on the head. "Hello, Nell-Bell," he said, quieter, but Avery heard it and her heart melted.

Even if things didn't work out between them, she knew this was the right move. Callum needed to be near Nell.

She was good for him. And he was good for her—even now, when Nell's fingers reached out and grabbed Callum's bottom lip.

"You didn't tell me you were planning a trip so soon. Is everything okay?" He frowned.

She smiled to reassure him. "More than okay."

He paused and then met Avery's eyes. She would swear he looked guilty of something. "You look good, Avery. Happy."

She was, she realized. Even with all the nerves and uncertainty, she was happy. In the time since leaving here in August, she'd discovered that she'd been trying to shoehorn herself into living someone else's life. She wasn't doing that anymore. Avery wasn't an afterthought or a surrogate anything. She was a single mom in charge of her own destiny.

Which brought her back to standing in front of Callum.

"I am happy. And I have some things to tell you. Mind if we come in?"

"Oh, of course!" He stood back, holding the door open for her to enter, Nell still sitting on his arm.

Callum's house hadn't fallen back into the same unkempt state as before, and she wondered if he had more time or if he'd kept on with the hired help from Butterfly House. It felt like home. And Callum's reception had been warmer than she'd expected, considering how they'd left things.

"You two sure gave me a surprise," he said, but Avery noticed he avoided looking into her eyes. Her heart sank, but only for a moment as he turned his attention back to his daughter. "How's my girl, huh?"

Nell giggled.

"Gosh, I missed her," he said. "I know it's only been a little over a month, but she's changed so much."

The sight of them together warmed Avery's heart. "She's sitting up on her own now. And I've had to start her on solid foods. She loves bananas and sweet potatoes."

Callum met her gaze. How she'd missed those dark, somber eyes. Was even more shocked when he reached out and took her hand with his free one.

"Avery, the day before you left…I was a complete ass. I should have apologized long ago but I could never find the right words. I'm so sorry for the things I said that morning."

It should have made what she had to say easier, but it didn't. "A lot happened in a short time," she said quietly. "I understood where it was coming from."

"You were right," he replied, his face close to Nell's. Goodness, they really did look alike. "I was scared and I lashed out at you."

He swallowed, and she saw his Adam's apple bob in his throat. She might as well go for broke and just say what she'd come to say. Someone had to break the silence. "Look, Callum, the reason we're here is because we've come to Cadence Creek to stay."

"You need a place to stay? Of course you should stay here." He still wasn't looking in her eyes, instead focused on his daughter, who had a death grip on his index finger.

Avery swallowed and tried again. "No, what I mean is…I've quit my job and terminated my lease and we've moved here for good."

That got his attention and his hand stopped moving. "You did what?"

He stared at her like she was crazy. Lord, this wasn't going as she expected. Then again, with Callum it never did, did it? The first time she'd arrived he'd called her a liar and slammed the door in her face, and she'd wanted nothing more than to return to her old life. Now here he was holding his daughter in his arms and she had uprooted everything so they could be together. Callum and Nell. Callum and her. All three of them.

And now that the moment was here she was absolutely terrified of telling him how she felt.

"It wasn't fair that Nell was so far away. You'd see her, what, maybe twice a year? With airfare being what it is… and let's face it, you can't up and move without selling your whole place. It was easier for me, and there are opportunities for me here. I saw that this summer when I had to turn down requests for private events."

"So you came for Nell. And for work. Is that it?"

She held his gaze, wanting to say the next words, the ones she'd practiced over and over in her head so often. They left her now, chased away by her fear of being turned away. He'd apologized but once more it fell short of any sort of declaration. She'd never laid her heart bare before anyone before, because she was always afraid it would get handed back. Not once in her life had anyone considered her worthy of fighting for. Not even Callum. He'd let her go so easily. Being the one to take the first step was terrifying.

"Don't you want to be closer to her?" she asked.

"Of course I do."

"Well, then."

"What are your plans?" he asked, settling Nell on his hip and reaching into a jug for a wooden spoon. He handed it to Nell to play with.

Disappointment rushed through her. That was all he was going to say about it? She struggled to keep her voice steady. "I'm renting the vacant spot next to the bakery. We're taking out the adjoining wall and joining forces. I'm going to specialize in cakes and cupcakes, and Jean and her staff are going to keep on with the breads and pies. We're adding a coffee area and some tables, too." She smiled. "Jean says we're going to give Martha Bullock at the Wagon Wheel a run for her money."

"It sounds great," he replied. "Well thought-out. Still. It's a big move, considering how much you loved your old job. To give up all that…"

Her throat tightened. "Nell needs her father. You were denied the opportunity to be a dad once before, Callum. I couldn't do that to you again."

Nell rapped his arm with the wooden spoon but he ignored her for once and pinned Avery with his gaze. "So this is about Jane?"

"Isn't it? I tried to tell you but you wouldn't believe me. I want to show you that not everyone is like her. Not everyone is out to deceive you or pretending to be something they're not. You couldn't believe the words, so I chose actions. I swear to God, Callum, I was as surprised by that feeling of relief as much as you were. Up to that point, I had believed wholeheartedly that Nell was absolutely yours. When I saw the results, I finally understood why you'd insisted on having the test in the first place. Concrete evidence."

"I overreacted that day," Callum admitted quietly. "What had happened between us scared me to death. I wanted to believe you. I did believe you. It was taking the next step that was freaking me out. It wasn't about Nell. It was about you and me."

Avery watched as he absently rubbed his broad hand over Nell's back. Nell was perfectly contented in his arms.

"You and Nell need each other."

"Yes, we do. But what about you, Avery? What do you need?"

She spun and looked out the window, surprised by the question and the rush of emotion it brought. "Oh, you know me. Just give me a decorating bag and a cake and I'm in my glory."

"Bull." He came to her then and finally, *finally,* touched her. He put his hand on her arm and spun her back to face him. She couldn't look in his face. If she did he'd see everything. So she stared at the button on his shirt instead.

"What do you need, Avery? Just say it."

"I need…"

She paused. Nothing had ever been this frightening before. Even with Crystal, she hadn't had a choice about the emotion or the heartbreak. This time, though, this was like putting her heart in her hands, passing it to Callum and giving him every opportunity to grind it beneath his heel.

"Yes?" he prompted, his fingers tightening on her sleeve.

"I need…"

Her breath clogged in her throat as she choked out an emotional hiccup. "I need you," she whispered.

"You need me," he repeated softly.

She nodded, tears spilling over her lashes. "Dammit," she lamented, wiping them off her cheeks. "I don't want to cry like an idiot. I don't want to…"

"What else, Avery? You need me…to do what?"

She shook her head. "This is so *hard,*" she whispered.

"I know," he answered. "God, I know. But I need you to say it, Avery. Please."

She took a big breath. "I need you to love me, Callum. Because I love you."

"Thank God," he murmured, letting out a giant breath.

"I didn't come back for work. I came back for you, Callum. And I'm so sorry for what happened before. So sorry how it all ended between us." Now that the words had started she couldn't seem to stop them. "My feelings for you were so new and scary, but it seemed like you didn't feel the same way. You were so cool about it all. So 'let's just take it slow and see what happens'. I made everything about Nell and we never talked about how we really felt, even after…"

She broke off, feeling suddenly awkward.

"After making love?"

She nodded.

He smiled softly. "That's why it hurt so much when I saw that look on your face when you read the results. We were together because I wanted to be with you. Because I found myself having feelings for you. I know I played it cool. That was my way of seeing if you were on the same page. It was all supposed to lead up to me asking you to stay. I was going to ask you that morning and then I just felt so…so foolish and betrayed."

"You were going to ask me to stay?"

He nodded. "When Jane told me the baby wasn't mine… you don't know what that did to me. It was ten times worse with Nell, because I already loved her. I'd held her in my arms and seen her smile and heard her laugh." He reached out with his hand and cupped her cheek. "I was afraid of everything I was feeling and that one little thing gave me the excuse I needed to lash out at you."

She lifted her eyes. "You were really going to ask me to stay here, with you?"

He nodded slowly. "I was going to ask you to do the very thing you're doing right now. Start your own business here in Cadence Creek. Not just because of Nell. Putting you on that plane, watching the two of you going through security was like watching my life walk away." He inched closer and his thumb began rubbing her cheekbone. "I want you here with me. I want to wake up in the morning with you beside me. I want Nell in her own room with her own crib. You made me start feeling again, made me face the past and remember all the dreams for the future I used to have. And what did I do? I freaked out and pushed you away."

He leaned forward and kissed her softly, the baby-powder scented shape of Nell between them, holding them slightly apart. Avery didn't mind. She had dreamed about kissing him again, longed for it in the depth of night when Nell was asleep and she'd felt incredibly lonely. Her life was broken into so many segments now. Before Crystal's death and after. Before Nell and after. Before falling in love with Callum…and after.

"What about the future you can have right now?" she asked, resting her forehead against his. "Do you trust me now, Callum?" She stepped back so she could look him in the face. "I know words aren't enough, but I'm trying to show you that I'm here, and that I'm ready to stick it out."

"As grand gestures go, it's pretty good," he admitted, a tender smile on his lips. It faded as his gaze plumbed hers. "I love you, Avery. I should have said so ages ago. I may have been angry, I may have been scared, but letting you walk away was the biggest mistake of my life."

He pulled back and nodded toward the door. "A mistake I was going to try to fix."

She turned and saw a packed duffel bag behind the door. "I don't understand."

His gaze delved into hers. "I hired one of the hands from Diamondback to watch things here for a few days. I was going to catch a flight to Toronto tonight." He sighed. "I was pretty sure I'd wrecked any chance between us. I gave up, just like you accused me of doing. It took me all of ten minutes to realize I'd been an idiot. Harder to swallow my pride, though, and face my fears dead-on. I certainly don't deserve another chance. But I knew I had to try. I love you, Avery. I love you so much. Nothing was right after you left."

"You were coming for me," she said softly, amazed.

"I was coming for you," he confirmed. "I should have done it sooner. I should never have let you go in the first place. How very like you to beat me to it." He smiled tenderly at her.

Avery swallowed around a lump in her throat. "Oh, Callum, you deserve so much more than you think. You deserve someone who loves you, who will be there for you. Who cares for the man you are rather than wishing you were someone else. I love you just as you are. You don't have to change a single thing."

His arms tightened around her, holding her so close that she wondered it was a miracle that Nell wasn't protesting by now. She breathed in the scent of the shampoo he used in the shower. It was the smell of home—the one she'd always been looking for and had never found.

"I love you," she repeated. There was no fear in the words. Instead they expanded into something big and bright and limitless. She smiled, tilting her head to look up into his face. His lips curved until they were grinning at each other and Nell was beating the spoon on his shoulder and saying "bah, bah," while neither of them cared a bit.

Callum kissed the top of her head, then rested his cheek on her hair. "You didn't give me the chance to show up with flowers and an apology. But I can't be sorry, not as long as you're here now..."

"Just try getting rid of me," she replied, snuggling into his side.

"Never," he decreed. "I won't let you walk away twice."

"Well, I'm not walking away now. I'm here to stay."

Callum released her from his embrace, handed Nell over

to her arms, then moved to stand in front of her. "Then I think we need to make it official."

"You do?"

Callum nodded. "Yes, I do. You should be *here,* Avery. You and Nell, in this house. It wasn't a home until you showed up and it's where you both belong. And since I don't expect this to be a temporary arrangement…"

He reached for her hand. "I don't have a ring or a fancy speech. All I can offer you is myself. So how about it? Will you marry me?"

"What happened to taking it slow?"

"I'm not letting you get away again. Not when I was so foolish to do it the first time. Marry me, Avery. Make us all a family."

Nell threw the spoon across the kitchen and it clattered on the floor, the sound making her throw up her hands and giggle.

Callum and Avery laughed at the surprised expression on Nell's face. Avery twined her fingers with his. She'd gone most of her life feeling like there was something missing. An anchor to keep her grounded. A safe place to rest her head and put down her worries. Here, in Cadence Creek and with Callum, she knew she'd found those missing pieces, and more. It wasn't easy, it wasn't perfect, but it was right. And she knew that whatever happened, they'd find a way to make it work…together.

"Yes," she answered, and let out a surprised squeak as Callum gathered her and Nell in his arms and lifted her to her toes.

When he put her down, she looked up at him beneath her lashes. "Callum?"

"Yes, sweetheart?"

She smiled softly. "If we're going to get married…I know Nell's not even a year old, but do you think…?"

His smile spread from ear to ear as he finished the sentence in his head. "Hell, yeah! You really want that?"

She hadn't known her heart could ever feel this full. "I always wanted a big family. And Nell will need brothers and sisters."

Callum let her go, went to the window and looked out for a moment. Avery held her breath. Was it too much all at once? Things had moved quickly. But she'd learned long ago that life was short. She'd wasted so much time; now she wanted to grab whatever happiness she could with both hands. She just hoped Callum felt the same....

He turned back and faced her, a satisfied smile on his lips. "Well, we're going to need to put in an addition," he said with a nonchalant shrug.

Avery went to him and lifted her face, inviting him to seal the agreement with a kiss. Several moments later, when Nell started to fuss, he whispered in her ear, "Is she due for a nap soon? Because I'd like to get started on that future we talked about."

The kitchen echoed with the warm laughter of family— and a couple in love.

* * * * *

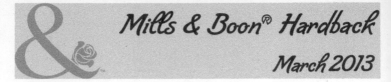
ROMANCE

Playing the Dutiful Wife	Carol Marinelli
The Fallen Greek Bride	Jane Porter
A Scandal, a Secret, a Baby	Sharon Kendrick
The Notorious Gabriel Diaz	Cathy Williams
A Reputation For Revenge	Jennie Lucas
Captive in the Spotlight	Annie West
Taming the Last Acosta	Susan Stephens
Island of Secrets	Robyn Donald
The Taming of a Wild Child	Kimberly Lang
First Time For Everything	Aimee Carson
Guardian to the Heiress	Margaret Way
Little Cowgirl on His Doorstep	Donna Alward
Mission: Soldier to Daddy	Soraya Lane
Winning Back His Wife	Melissa McClone
The Guy To Be Seen With	Fiona Harper
Why Resist a Rebel?	Leah Ashton
Sydney Harbour Hospital: Evie's Bombshell	Amy Andrews
The Prince Who Charmed Her	Fiona McArthur

MEDICAL

NYC Angels: Redeeming The Playboy	Carol Marinelli
NYC Angels: Heiress's Baby Scandal	Janice Lynn
St Piran's: The Wedding!	Alison Roberts
His Hidden American Beauty	Connie Cox

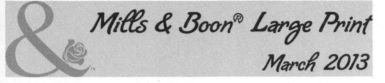

Mills & Boon® Large Print

March 2013

ROMANCE

A Night of No Return	Sarah Morgan
A Tempestuous Temptation	Cathy Williams
Back in the Headlines	Sharon Kendrick
A Taste of the Untamed	Susan Stephens
The Count's Christmas Baby	Rebecca Winters
His Larkville Cinderella	Melissa McClone
The Nanny Who Saved Christmas	Michelle Douglas
Snowed in at the Ranch	Cara Colter
Exquisite Revenge	Abby Green
Beneath the Veil of Paradise	Kate Hewitt
Surrendering All But Her Heart	Melanie Milburne

HISTORICAL

How to Sin Successfully	Bronwyn Scott
Hattie Wilkinson Meets Her Match	Michelle Styles
The Captain's Kidnapped Beauty	Mary Nichols
The Admiral's Penniless Bride	Carla Kelly
Return of the Border Warrior	Blythe Gifford

MEDICAL

Her Motherhood Wish	Anne Fraser
A Bond Between Strangers	Scarlet Wilson
Once a Playboy…	Kate Hardy
Challenging the Nurse's Rules	Janice Lynn
The Sheikh and the Surrogate Mum	Meredith Webber
Tamed by her Brooding Boss	Joanna Neil

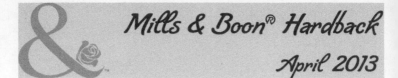

ROMANCE

Master of her Virtue	Miranda Lee
The Cost of her Innocence	Jacqueline Baird
A Taste of the Forbidden	Carole Mortimer
Count Valieri's Prisoner	Sara Craven
The Merciless Travis Wilde	Sandra Marton
A Game with One Winner	Lynn Raye Harris
Heir to a Desert Legacy	Maisey Yates
The Sinful Art of Revenge	Maya Blake
Marriage in Name Only?	Anne Oliver
Waking Up Married	Mira Lyn Kelly
Sparks Fly with the Billionaire	Marion Lennox
A Daddy for Her Sons	Raye Morgan
Along Came Twins…	Rebecca Winters
An Accidental Family	Ami Weaver
A Date with a Bollywood Star	Riya Lakhani
The Proposal Plan	Charlotte Phillips
Their Most Forbidden Fling	Melanie Milburne
The Last Doctor She Should Ever Date	Louisa George

MEDICAL

NYC Angels: Unmasking Dr Serious	Laura Iding
NYC Angels: The Wallflower's Secret	Susan Carlisle
Cinderella of Harley Street	Anne Fraser
You, Me and a Family	Sue MacKay

Mills & Boon® Large Print
April 2013

ROMANCE

A Ring to Secure His Heir	Lynne Graham
What His Money Can't Hide	Maggie Cox
Woman in a Sheikh's World	Sarah Morgan
At Dante's Service	Chantelle Shaw
The English Lord's Secret Son	Margaret Way
The Secret That Changed Everything	Lucy Gordon
The Cattleman's Special Delivery	Barbara Hannay
Her Man in Manhattan	Trish Wylie
At His Majesty's Request	Maisey Yates
Breaking the Greek's Rules	Anne McAllister
The Ruthless Caleb Wilde	Sandra Marton

HISTORICAL

Some Like It Wicked	Carole Mortimer
Born to Scandal	Diane Gaston
Beneath the Major's Scars	Sarah Mallory
Warriors in Winter	Michelle Willingham
A Stranger's Touch	Anne Herries

MEDICAL

A Socialite's Christmas Wish	Lucy Clark
Redeeming Dr Riccardi	Leah Martyn
The Family Who Made Him Whole	Jennifer Taylor
The Doctor Meets Her Match	Annie Claydon
The Doctor's Lost-and-Found Heart	Dianne Drake
The Man Who Wouldn't Marry	Tina Beckett